HOLLY JOLLY DREAMS

Mistletoe Meadows
Book 5

JESSIE GUSSMAN

Contents

Acknowledgments

Cover art by Covers and Cupcakes
Editing by Heather Hayden
Narration by Jay Dyess
Author Services by CE Author Assistant

Listen to the unabridged audio for FREE performed by Jay Dyess on the Say with Jay channel on YouTube. Get early access to all of Jay's recordings and listen to Jessie's books before they're available to the general public, plus get daily Bible readings by Jay and bonus scenes by becoming a Say with Jay channel member.

Chapter One

"Wait a second, you are the Secret Saint?" Roland McBride slammed the tree down in the back of his pickup and stopped what he was doing to stare at his brother-in-law. It was almost midnight, and there wasn't a whole lot of light from the dim pole lights in the tree farm parking lot, but he could clearly see his brother-in-law, Judd, nodding.

"Yeah. I had the torch passed to me by someone who wishes to remain anonymous, but yeah. I was the Secret Saint, and your sister and I did it for a while."

Roland nodded. It didn't surprise him at all that his sister had been involved in it. She was a kind and caring soul, which was part of the reason she'd become a doctor.

"But with getting married and with Terry and me taking on more responsibilities and we thought that children might come..." Judd smiled a little bit, and Roland wondered exactly what that meant. Could Terry and Judd be expecting?

He supposed they'd announce it when they felt like the time was right. In the meantime, he listened as Judd continued. "If you're not interested, that's fine. It just seems like you're perfect for the role. You've got tons of connections, and of course, Terry and I would help you. With her job as a doctor, she sees all kinds and hears a lot. She was a great help to me before I passed the torch."

"You're talking like you're not the Secret Saint anymore. Is that right?"

"That's correct, but it's not up to me to give the identities of the people who are doing it now. Just know that their situations have changed, similar to mine, and they need to step back. We can all continue to do it, but it would be nice to have someone who would totally take over."

Judd didn't say it, but what he really meant was someone who was single, who didn't have a lot of family responsibilities, who had some extra money and no children or wife to spend it on.

Roland understood. And it frustrated him a little bit. But Judd was right, and he couldn't argue with that.

"No, I'm definitely interested." Maybe this would give his life some purpose. He felt a little bit like he was drifting lately with all of his siblings finding love and getting married.

Of course, there was Isadora, who had found love, so she thought, had three children with her love, and then had her husband cheat and leave her. He supposed she wasn't quite in the same boat as he was. At least she had children and had the opportunity to experience marriage.

"I don't want to push you into anything you don't want to do," Judd said as he lifted another Christmas tree and put it on the back of Roland's truck.

Roland ran the family Christmas tree farm and got most of his income from that, although he did work as a handyman the rest of the year.

"No, I've got to say that it's an honor to be chosen. I really feel that it is, and I'm flattered you think that I can do it."

"We definitely think that you can. We know that you can. But it does take up an awful lot of one's time, and while I know that you have the love for other people that the job requires, it can really cut into your Christmas season."

Another reason why it would be best for the Secret Saint to be a single person, Roland was sure, although Judd did not say that.

"Thank you for the vote of confidence."

"If you need some time to think about it, that's fine."

"No, I don't need to think about it. I'm sure this is something I definitely want to do." Again, he thought it might give his life some purpose, give him the feeling that he was getting up for something. Lately, things had just been—not exactly in a depressive state, but he just wondered what the purpose was. Why was he living? Sure, he had nieces and nephews he loved to spend time with, and he felt like he was as good an uncle as an uncle could be, but was that really all there was going to be to his life?

Mistletoe Meadows was not exactly a huge town, and if he hadn't already found his lifetime love, there wasn't a whole lot of opportunity for him to meet someone new.

He really wanted to do something with his life, to have some kind of significance other than being the baby of the McBride family.

"A lot of times, we find our purpose in serving others. You already do that as an uncle, and Terry and I have often commented on how selfless you are with your nieces and nephews."

He hadn't realized that anyone had noticed, and he certainly hadn't done it for notoriety.

"Well, thank you, although I certainly didn't do it for attention or accolades. But there definitely is a certain satisfaction in doing kind things for others, especially when it requires a sacrifice from oneself."

"Exactly. Terry talks about that all the time in her work, whether it's saving someone's life or something as simple as helping bring a child's fever down. The idea that her work has meaning gives meaning to her own life."

"Good for her," Roland said, and he didn't mean that in an offhanded, flippant way. He really did think that Terry had deliberately chosen her profession for that very reason, because she knew that it would give meaning to her life and help others. Terry was just that kind of person.

"So we can count on you?"

"You sure can. You'll just have to let me know what to do."

"Sometimes that's the hardest thing of all, but Terry and I have a bit of a list of things and people that we've noticed around town." Judd pulled a list out of his back pocket as Roland slammed another Christmas tree onto the back of the truck.

It was just after Thanksgiving, and that was the busiest time of year for the tree farm, sales-wise anyway.

People who came to get their trees came all through the month of December, with Christmas Eve being one of their busiest shopping days.

Judd shook out the paper, and it rattled and crinkled.

Roland took off his glove and grasped the sheet.

They had yet to get their first snow of the season, but the air was crisp and cool, well below freezing. If there had been any precipitation in the forecast, it would definitely have come down as the white stuff.

"Wow. That's quite a list."

"Don't feel like you have to do everything, and don't feel like you can't ask for help. A lot of times, businesses are more than happy to donate if you mention that it's for the Secret Saint, and you can get other people to ask for you, so it's not you going around bringing a lot of attention to yourself. Terry helps, and your mom is really awesome, although she's slowed down in recent years."

Roland nodded. His mother was getting older. She was sixty now, and he supposed that slowing down was normal, although it was hard for him to picture his energetic, perpetually happy mother as anything other than elbows deep in whatever was going on around her.

"So I could go to you?" Roland asked.

"Yes. Me, your sister, your mother. I don't know that I would ask too many other people, because the more people you bring in, the more chance you have of being found out, and," Judd smiled, "well, that would not be the end of the world, but it is nice to have that element of mystery. It makes a nicer story and gets people involved and talking. If everyone knew who did it, it would kind of be one of those things that are just the way they are, you know?"

"Yes, I can totally see the value of keeping it a secret." That wasn't hard at all. Even a guy like himself could see that.

"All right then, you can take a look at the list. You don't have to go over it now, because I know you're busy—you've got to get these trees delivered before six—but tomorrow when you have time, take a look at it and see if there's anything there that you think you can do. If you need resources, whether it's money or groceries or building supplies, check with me, and I'll see what I can do. I have a network who knows that I work with the Secret Saint, but they know it's not me. I've been very careful since I stopped to make sure that I am seen while the Secret Saint is on the other side of town doing something. That way, I'm a great contact person but not someone who is under suspicion."

"That's wise," Roland said. Judd seemed to have everything figured out, and he had to admit that he was impressed.

They finished loading the trees, and Judd left while Roland got in the truck and spent the next few hours delivering them. By the time he got in, he was too tired to look at the list, although he set it on his dresser.

He lived with his mom, and he felt like he was a blessing to his mom as much as she was a blessing to him. Ever since their dad passed away, he had helped take care of all of the things outside and the upkeep of the house. Being that he was a pretty good handyman, he had completely redone their porch and installed new windows when the window seals around the current windows had started to rot out. He made sure she had plenty of firewood and provided fuel for the backup oil furnace. He also cleaned the chimney every year and did all the yard and outside maintenance.

He supposed if someone wanted to make fun of him for being thirty and still living with his mom, they could go ahead and do that, but it had always been his job to take care of her and the property after each of his siblings had left. He kind of liked the idea that it was his responsibility to take care of their mom. He also felt like he probably knew her better than any of his other siblings, especially now. But maybe that was the reason why only he seemed to notice that something more than just a little slowing down was happening, at least from what he could see.

Or maybe his position made him worry a little more about her.

Chapter Two

"That's so nice that you're able to take me, and I don't have to drive myself. I really hate driving after dark nowadays," Marjorie McBride said to Roland as they pulled up to Gilbert and Summer's new home.

Gilbert and Summer had just gotten married, and Lucas, Marissa, and Robert, Gilbert's children with his first wife, were adjusting well to their new stepmother.

The couple loved their new home and enjoyed hosting meals for everyone in the family.

It was tradition to have Sunday dinner after church at Marjorie's house, although Roland worried that it might be getting to be too much for her. Still, he hadn't said anything. But since Sunday dinner was taken care of, Gilbert and Summer often had something on a Friday night.

All their siblings were present, even Isadora, who had moved back in with Marjorie and Roland and looked terrible. It had been a while, more than a year, since her husband had left her, and emotionally she seemed to have gotten over it, but physically she had lost weight, and she just seemed completely exhausted from taking care of her children and trying to work full-time as well.

"Welcome, come on in," Summer said as they got to the door. They hadn't even gotten to knock, which typically they just knocked and then walked in calling out that they were coming.

"That was pretty good timing," Roland said as he took his mother's elbow and held the door for his mother to go in first. Marjorie might not be hosting the meal at her house, but she had brought plenty of food to go around. Roland was carrying the dessert that she had made.

"It smells amazing in here," Marjorie said, and it seemed like she sounded a little out of breath. Roland looked at her carefully. Was she pale?

"Thanks. The chicken pad Thai nachos really make the house smell delicious. And it's a perfect meal for a lot of people." She grinned. "Okay, maybe it's a perfect meal for kids, because it's basically finger food."

Roland laughed along with her, but there was a part of him that wished that he knew what exactly was a good meal for kids, but since he didn't have any of his own... He felt like he was missing out a little.

"Did Isadora drive herself?" Summer said as she closed the door behind them.

"She's coming shortly. She had to stop in town and pick up a couple of supplies for one of the projects that her kids are supposed to make for school."

"Uncle Roland!" Lucas, Marissa, and Robert called as they came out of the kitchen.

He balanced the dessert in one hand and held out his other arm for them to come and give him a hug.

As the children got older, they probably would outgrow the whole idea of running to him and wrapping their arms around him, but until they did, he was going to enjoy it.

"We're so glad you're here!" Robert said.

"Are you going to play with us after we eat?" Marissa asked.

"We'll see. It's pretty chilly out, and your mom might not want you to be out too late either, depending on what you have to do this weekend."

"I have clients in the morning, so the kids can sleep in if they want to," Summer said.

He knew she still gave horseback riding lessons, and he nodded.

The kids chatted around them as they walked into the kitchen.

Then Robert said, "I do have to work on a project. I'm in Miss Bushnell's class, and she always has the most fun projects. But I want to beat Kylie, who always thinks she's so great at everything." Robert sneered at the idea that Kylie was actually good at anything.

"Well, I've got some things I need to do, but I can give you a hand if you want me to."

"That would be awesome! You always have the best ideas. The last time you and I made the race car track, that was the coolest thing ever. Miss Bushnell was really impressed. She said that no one had ever made anything like that before."

"Wow. I'm so glad we could impress your teacher." Roland tried not to let the idea that Miss Bushnell was actually Nelly, his sworn enemy from third grade, take root in his mind. After all, a lot of years had gone by since the whole valentine incident, when she got so angry at him and swore that they would never speak again. Surely she was over it, although...they really hadn't ever spoken again since then.

They had been sworn enemies, and he had to admit that he had kind of gotten involved in it more than maybe was totally appropriate.

But that was back when he was a kid in school. He was beyond that now.

Although, mention of her name still made his lip curl.

"Hey, I'm here," Isadora called from the doorway. Her kids tripped in ahead of her as she carried a bag of what looked like potato chips.

"I didn't bake anything, but I thought I had to contribute to the meal somehow," she said, looking tired as she held up a bag of chips.

"You didn't have to bring anything," Summer said as she went and took the bag from Isadora before giving her a hug. "I'm so glad you're here."

Roland wished she wouldn't have brought anything. It was enough for her to be trying to raise three kids by herself and work full-time, trying to get as many hours as she could while her kids were either sleeping or at school.

"Are you guys gonna come in so we can eat sometime soon?" Judd asked from where he stood with Terry at the dining room.

He was joking, of course, but the family made their way into the room, taking that as a hint, since everyone really was hungry.

Amy and her husband, Jones, along with Wilson and Charity, were already in there. Amy and Jones, best friends since they were little, were bickering back and forth. That hadn't stopped since they'd gotten married. But usually, their arguments ended in a kiss now, which was new.

Wilson was a wonderful dad to Charity's five children. It looked like they had just announced that they were expecting another baby.

Charity seemed to glow with her pregnancy, and Wilson never stopped touching her, whether it was a hand on her arm or an arm around her shoulder. It made Roland wish that he had someone to be protective of, to be caring for, to look out for and take care of.

The family gathered around the table, laughing and teasing each other, with the kids being loud but not obnoxious. The feeling of family rolled over him, and he was grateful that his family had stayed close and that they still got together regularly. But it also made him feel strikingly alone. After all, he was the only one in his family who hadn't been married and didn't have at least a child to keep him company.

Other than maybe his mother. But he still lived at her house—did that count?

He watched her, smiling and talking, but...he couldn't escape the nagging feeling that there was something wrong.

Still, after the meal was over, everyone helped clear the dishes, and they played a few games and enjoyed talking with each other before it was time to leave.

"I don't know what I'm going to do when you have a family of your own and I have to go by myself to these things. I might depend on someone to pick me up."

"Maybe when I have a family of my own, I'll just live with you," Roland said easily. He figured that his mom feared change. And he also figured that there wasn't much chance of him having a family of his own. After all, who was he going to marry?

"You know you're welcome anytime. I have always appreciated the work you've done to help with the upkeep of the home through the years. I don't know what I would have done without you, although I do know that God would have provided. Still, the provision that He gave was you, and I am deeply grateful." His mom smiled at him across the seat, and he glanced over and smiled back at her.

Maybe she was just getting old. And that made him sad too. But maybe it was best that he didn't have a family—that way he was able to do his best to help his mother. He didn't have anyone holding him back or getting in his way. That was the reason he was a good choice for the Secret Saint.

Speaking of which, he knew that tonight after he got home, he would help his mom inside and make sure she got to bed. He would wait until he was sure that she was asleep, and then he would slip out.

It took a little longer than what he thought, since his mom seemed to be restless, getting up twice—once to go to the bathroom and once to get a drink. She saw him still sitting on a stool in the kitchen and came out to chat.

Thankfully, she didn't come around the bar, or she might have seen that he had already put his boots on and was just making sure that he didn't hear anything else from her.

They chatted for a bit, and she went back to bed.

He supposed, according to what Judd had said, that it really didn't matter if his mom found out that he was the Secret Saint, but still, in the interest of keeping it as much of a secret as he could, he wasn't going to tell her.

He wondered, after speaking with Judd and realizing that Judd wasn't the first Secret Saint, who the actual first Secret Saint had been.

Maybe they were dead and gone, since he couldn't really remember any Secret Saint activities before Judd had begun.

Tonight, he had decided to deliver groceries to the Harney family. They were on the list that Judd had given him, as being in need, and groceries were a pretty easy way to get started.

Roland had to admit he was excited about it as he drove to the box store, which was an hour away from Mistletoe Meadows. He had to go up and down three mountains, around hairpin turns, and finally down into the town of Whisker Hollow. He grabbed the groceries that he needed and made the harrowing trip back.

He loved where he lived—the views were amazing, and the wide-open meadows were bordered by thousands of acres of mountain woods. It was the best of all worlds and a little cooler than the rest of the low-lying Virginia area. They almost had northern weather, they joked among themselves at times. But he didn't mind, because it meant snow at Christmas, and he really loved that.

Thankfully, it wasn't snowing tonight, or that would have made this trip treacherous with all of the steep hills and curves.

It was almost two o'clock in the morning before he arrived at the Harney house. Actually, he parked down the street from them and made four trips, carrying two bags of groceries in each hand as he did so.

On the last trip, as he settled the groceries down, he noticed something he hadn't noticed before.

Two bags, similar to his but sitting inside a box with the top cut off it, sat right next to the door.

That was odd.

Realizing that he had been smelling freshly baked bread, and the smell hadn't penetrated his consciousness, he wondered if the freshly baked bread could be in the bags?

It was just the way it was all placed, and it made him wonder if someone else was doing something kind for the Harneys.

Not that the Harneys couldn't use any kind of good at all. From what he understood, they could use all the help they could get.

But still, he was about to creep forward, just to put his nose next to the box to see if what he suspected was actually true, when the porch light snapped on.

Thankfully, he was standing beside a big old oak tree in the middle of the yard, and he ducked behind it quickly.

Judd hadn't mentioned it, but perhaps a ski mask would be a good idea from here on out. And a special coat that he wore only when he was making Secret Saint deliveries. That way, if someone did happen to see him, they couldn't have any kind of identifying information on him.

"Did you hear something?" someone from inside the house said as the door opened.

"I thought I heard a thump," a man's voice answered.

Mr. Harney had had an accident the previous year at work, and he hadn't been able to go back to his regular job. The job that he was working now wasn't nearly enough to keep his family of eight children fed, hence the need for help.

"What's that?" the woman's voice said, and the door opened wider as the man bent down and picked up the box with the bags in it.

They hadn't noticed the groceries yet, and it made Roland itchy. He wanted them to see the groceries. *Come on, look at the edge of the porch. There's a lot more than just two little bags.*

But they were examining the bags that they had found. He could hear the paper crinkling from where he stood behind the tree.

He made sure that nothing more than his forehead and nose were sticking out as he watched the people opening up the bags.

"Oh my goodness! It's freshly baked bread!"

"It's still warm," Mr. Harney said.

"I wonder who could have done that? Wow. We could have that for breakfast."

"If we keep making all of this noise, the kids will be up and we can have it now."

He didn't sound like that was such a terrible thing. The bread must smell really good and inviting.

"George, what's that?" the woman said.

Mr. Harney's gaze followed to where her finger pointed.

"Maybe more fresh baked bread?" he asked, and the hope in his voice was unmistakable.

Roland's stomach fell. They were going to be sorely disappointed if they were expecting eight bags of freshly baked bread.

Suddenly, he didn't like the idea of being a Secret Saint, especially if people weren't going to appreciate what he did.

But that was wrong, wasn't it? The idea of working for man's applause rather than God's praise. He knew what he had done was good and necessary, and it shouldn't matter whether or not it was appreciated.

He stopped thinking about that when the woman said, "Oh my goodness, George. These are groceries. Someone left us eight bags of groceries!" she said, the excitement in her voice making it tremble. Her hands went to her cheeks.

"Oh, George. I didn't know how I was going to afford the groceries, with the money that I had to put back to pay for Riley's braces. Oh my goodness. This is amazing." She turned and started going through the bags without even picking them up.

"It's everything that we could possibly need. Plus a few little extra things. Look at this! Some treats for the kids. And a six-pack of your favorite energy drink. Who would have thought to get the exact kind that you like?" She sounded amazed.

Roland silently thanked God that he had picked out the right kind. He hadn't had a clue, other than he remembered seeing Mr. Harney standing beside the gas station in town, an energy drink in hand. He hadn't had the slightest idea of which one it was.

Lord, You knew. You guided my hands to the right one. Thank you.

It was amazing and so satisfying to see their excitement and the emotion that they displayed.

He wanted to slip quietly away, but he was stuck behind the tree until they carried all the groceries in. Then, it seemed like a couple of the kids had gotten up, and he could see heads moving around the kitchen as the groceries came out on the table, and the kids peppered them with questions.

That was when he slipped away, feeling very satisfied, although there was still a nagging feeling in his heart. Who had left the bread?

Chapter Three

"Even though you're young, there are always things that you can do to help out." Nelly Bushnell stood in front of her third-grade classroom after closing the book that she had just been reading.

Nothing made her happier than to hear her classroom completely and totally silent, despite the fact that they were wiggly, squirmy eight-year-olds who had more energy than should be legal, and listen raptly to her reading.

It was a book that she had enjoyed when she was young, and she loved reading it to her students. Not just because it was a great, entertaining story, although it was, but because there were so many lessons to be learned.

"Yes, Robert?" she said as Robert McBride raised his hand. He had been making great strides since the beginning of the year, when he was still a little down about his mother's death, and was so much better than last year, when he had been devastated. She was thankful for Summer, who had walked into that family and been a blessing in every way, becoming the children's stepmom not long ago.

"I help my Uncle Roland with the Christmas trees. He gives a lot away."

"That's very nice, Robert," Nelly said, not making any other comment but calling on another student immediately and listening as they spoke.

The mention of Roland McBride made her want to curl her lip. She and Roland had been enemies ever since the valentine incident.

She supposed she was too old for such shenanigans, but he had been her sworn, lifetime enemy, and they had never reconciled.

Maybe part of her actually enjoyed having a sworn enemy, but most of her just thought that Roland was a selfish, immature brat who never grew up.

But she loved the rest of his family.

As always happened after she read the book, the classroom was abuzz with ideas and ways that the children could help, despite their age. They had a robust conversation before she quieted everyone down to take out their English books and began to teach about nouns and verbs.

She tried to make her lessons interesting and interactive as much as possible. She had never had a problem sitting still in school, but she understood that some kids, especially boys, did. And especially so in this age of digital stimulation where attention spans were about an eighth of a millimeter long.

It made teaching harder and harder, although she did use some electronics in her lesson plans. Just because that was the way the world was going.

She tried to teach the old-fashioned way as much as she possibly could, because she thought it was good for the students to learn to pay attention and listen to real, live, actual humans.

"Robert, would you like to read the sentence that you made up for your homework," she said, calling on Robert McBride again.

"Sure. Uncle Roland helped me with this, and we came up with, 'The Christmas tree fell down.'"

She asked him what the noun in the sentence was and then to

name the verb. He actually had an action verb, which made her lesson easier to explain.

But the mention of Roland had her mind going back to the year she was in third grade, thinking of her eight-year-old self making a valentine for the school exchange. She had a huge crush on Tommy Peterson that year and had made his extra special, with lots of hearts, and she even attempted to draw them herself. She was such a romantic, even back then. Unfortunately, instead of Tommy getting his card, somehow Roland ended up with it. He had made a huge deal about it, showing it to everyone and laughing at her ridiculous romanticism.

She had been completely humiliated, and she had declared him her enemy for life. She had sworn that night at home in her bed with the covers over her head and tears streaming down her face that she would always beat Roland at everything.

And she had. From that moment on, whether it was a foot race—she was faster than he was—or a test score where she got a better grade, she made it her mission to always, always beat Roland.

Perhaps her childhood was still influencing her adult behavior, since, while she loved Robert, he was one of her favorite students—if a teacher could actually admit to having favorites—she absolutely hated every time he mentioned Roland's name and had a physical reaction that she had to take pains to hide.

It was something she was working on, she assured herself as she walked into the house she shared with her grandmother that evening.

She set her bag down by the door, at the entrance to the living room. She would sit in the living room later this evening after supper and grade the papers she brought home with her that she hadn't gotten done during her planning period, because she spent most of it talking to Jillian and Cara about how they needed to bury the hatchet and get along.

The entire time, she had been thinking about her competition with Roland that lasted all through her elementary school, junior high, and high school years. If they had gone to the same college, she was sure it would have lasted through that as well.

Actually, she wasn't sure Roland ever went to college.

As the youngest McBride, he was the one that was left to take care of the Christmas tree farm after his dad had died. She supposed she should have felt bad for him.

"I've been looking for my car keys all day, and I just cannot find them. I have a hair appointment, and I'm late," her grandmother said as she wandered into the kitchen. She wore her nightgown and slippers.

"Grandma," she said as she walked over. Her grandmother had been having more and more periods of confusion, which she supposed meant dementia at her age.

"Nelly, oh my goodness. Is it time for you to be home already? How was college today?"

"It was fine, Grandma," she said, wondering whether she should correct her but knowing from experience that if she did, it usually just made things worse. Her grandma didn't get upset per se, she just...got insistent that she was right.

Nelly supposed it was her stubborn streak coming out. Grandma had always talked about her stubbornness and how she had worked to overcome it. But maybe, as a person's mind got older and dementia took over, they were no longer able to suppress some of the things that they had worked to overcome in their younger years. That was the only thing that Nelly could figure out, since her grandma had always been sweet and an absolutely amazing person for her entire life. Someone she had been able to lean on.

In fact, Grandma was the one who had sat down beside her bed and petted her head and wiped away her tears when she cried over her valentine to Tommy Peterson. Her grandmother was the one who had suggested that instead of being hurt and upset about it, she use it to make herself better, perhaps by challenging herself to rise to a higher standard.

She doubted that her grandma meant to inspire a lifelong

competition between Nelly and Roland, although that's what had happened.

"Grandma, you just got your hair done. I think you're confused about what week it is," she said, not mentioning that Grandma had had her keys taken away from her two years prior and that there was no hair appointment scheduled for at least six weeks.

"My goodness. Time flies, doesn't it?" her grandma said, laughing softly.

"It sure does," Nelly said, believing that with her whole heart. How was it that she was already thirty years old? Time flew so quickly, and she couldn't believe that her twenties were over. When did that happen?

"I worry about you sometimes, my dear," her grandma said as they moved to the counter where the food that she had put in the crockpot that morning gave the entire house a delicious aroma that made coming home a joy.

"You don't need to worry about me, Grandma. I have you."

"But you should have someone special. Someone who loves you for just who you are." Her grandma smiled. "Someone like my Stuart."

Her grandma's love affair with Stuart was well known in Mistletoe Meadows. Although it had been years since Grandpa died, Nelly still remembered him with fondness. He always had a twinkle in his eye and a joke to tell, as well as a harmonica in his pocket, which he would pull out at random times to play a song and get a smile from someone.

She had loved that when she was younger, just enjoying the ability to pull a song out of one's pocket. And that ability to give a smile to anyone at any time. She had learned a lot from her grandpa, even though she hadn't had a lot of time with him. He definitely instilled in her the desire to make people smile.

She went to the crockpot and reached above it to get plates out.

She remembered that she hadn't run the dishwasher the day before because she had been thinking she would put the supper dishes in, and then she'd been too exhausted after grading papers all evening to come back to the kitchen and finish her work.

"Are you okay, honey?" Grandma said from behind her.

Nelly took a breath, straightening her shoulders. She probably shouldn't have taken on yet another responsibility, but jumping in as a Secret Saint had been too irresistible for her to pass up. She was in a unique position, because of her classroom, and the children were at an age where they still told everything without realizing that some things maybe were a little bit more personal. So she knew lots of people who could use help over the holidays, and she couldn't resist.

Plus, her house was paid for, since she lived with her grandma, and she had plenty of money for herself, so why not spread smiles around? Just like her grandpa.

But it did leave her tired—teaching all day and taking care of her grandma in the evening.

They did have a home health aide who came and spent a few hours with her grandma every day, but perhaps it was time to do a bit more than that since her grandma's episodes of confusion were getting more and more common.

The one today had scared her just a bit.

"Are you ready to eat?" she asked Grandma as she put the dishes in the sink and began to wash them.

"I'm hungry. I didn't think you'd ever get home," Grandma said, sounding like her old self. "I should have washed those for you. I didn't even notice they were in there."

Normally, her grandma would have noticed, but that was just one more thing that was changing.

Nelly's heart ached a bit at the idea that her grandma wasn't ever going to be the same. It was hard to think about.

But she was determined to keep her home as long as possible, because that's what Grandma had said she wanted, and even now when she was in her right mind, it was what she would say. But the responsibility was almost overwhelming.

Later that night, after her grandmother had gone to bed and she had finished grading her papers and made sure that she had gotten all the dishes in the dishwasher and had it started so she wouldn't have to wash dishes before they could eat tomorrow, Nelly pulled out the necessary items that she had purchased the last weekend when she had gone to the big box store and started organizing them into food baskets. She imagined the families' reactions and wished that she could have been there when the Harneys had seen their fresh baked bread. She had deliberately taken her early morning walk by their house, just so she could see them opening their door and the smiles on their faces, but the bread had been gone. Obviously, she hadn't gotten up early enough, or she made too much noise when she dropped it off on their porch and woke them up the night before.

She didn't think she had. She had taken a lot of care to be quiet, but...maybe she'd been louder than what she thought. After all, she'd been a little preoccupied, thinking about making people smile and doing good deeds, just like the Bible said. To not let your right hand know what your left hand was doing, but to do your good deeds without thought of reward for yourself, knowing that God would reward you.

She wasn't even necessarily doing it for the rewards, although she knew God saw everything. She was doing it just because it made her feel good. Because she knew that it made God smile to see His children being kind and doing good to others.

She finished packaging the food baskets and grabbed the cloak that she used particularly for these deliveries. It was a cloak that used to belong to her grandmother, where the hood came well over her hair and completely hid her face from view. The cloak flowed down to her knees and hid her figure as well. She could hide a lot of things in the folds of the cloak, and she loved it, since it was also warm and comfortable as well.

She walked outside, carrying all four baskets under her cloak and humming softly to herself.

It wasn't super late, but she knew it was late enough that most people would be inside. Especially considering that it was so cold out.

She saw some other people coming down the sidewalk and ducked into a woodshed before they saw her. While she wasn't afraid of being recognized, she did try to avoid people as much as she could.

She stood in the darkness as they came closer.

"I wanted to take a walk outside tonight, because I heard the Harney family had an unexpected surprise this week."

She smiled to herself as the people got closer and she could hear them talking about the gift that she had given.

"I heard that too! Eight bags of groceries! Oh my goodness, that must have been four hundred dollars. Who has that kind of money to just give to someone else?"

Wait. Eight bags of groceries? That wasn't what she gave them. It was two loaves of bread.

Immediately she thought about the miracle in the scriptures where Jesus had turned two fishes and five loaves of bread into enough food to feed five thousand people. Surely he hadn't changed her two loaves of bread into eight bags of groceries?

She was trying to reconcile the idea of that in her brain, and come up with a scientific explanation for it, when the person said, "I just thought maybe we'd run into someone doing something suspicious. After all, I know the Harneys would really like to thank them, and I have a few people I know who could use some help." They went on to mention a few people, some that Nelly knew from her classroom and some that she made a mental note to research.

"I think they got something else too besides the groceries. Was it bread or something?" the other person said.

So her bread hadn't experienced a miracle of God. Of course not.

Then, the truth struck. Someone else was doing Secret Saint activities! Who could this person be?

She knew there had been Secret Saint activities the year before, but up until Nelly had started, nothing had been done. She assumed that whoever had been the Secret Saint had either moved away or retired from their activities. It was rather expensive, and she could understand that they probably couldn't do it year after year.

But this—this having someone do the same family on the same night that she had... It felt like someone was spying on her or deliberately trying to steal her thunder and outdo her.

Well, she wouldn't allow that to happen. She would have to find out who this other Secret Saint was. Figure out who they were targeting, and make sure that she outdid them.

That wasn't exactly the correct attitude she should have, and it didn't sit totally well with her, but her competitive spirit was in full force, and as the people walked by, and she slipped out of the woodshed, delivering her baskets, she determined that she would figure things out.

When she got home, she got onto the town's social media website. They kept things updated and had provided an ongoing tracker of the Secret Saint. Nelly hadn't been paying too much attention to it this year, after she realized that there wasn't anything to report.

Now, she saw that indeed, her bread had been received, but there was also mention of other things that she hadn't done.

It was the other Secret Saint, and as she studied the social media posts, she thought she could find a pattern.

She needed to be more systematic about her giving and outdo whoever was competing with her. In the meantime, it definitely called for further investigation.

Chapter Four

"was really hoping we could talk about what we're going to do this year. It's always good to get some plans in before things get too wild, and we end up not being able to find a day that works for everyone." Marjorie sat at the head of the table, looking down at all of her children.

Roland loved these dinners and enjoyed the time to get together with his family. But it also was a really great time to hear who needed help. He certainly was listening to conversations with a different ear than he used to.

Summer, who had removed some of the food from the table, sat back down.

"We should be able to do whatever works for everyone else. Once school is out, all of the school things are over, and we should have two weeks that are mostly unbroken except for the three days we're going to spend at Wilson's in-laws." Charity listed those dates, and Marjorie jotted them down in a little notebook that she had.

Anyone else might have used their phone, but Marjorie was still old school. His mother had little notes stuck all around the house. Notes about gifts she was giving, and things that she had bought, and things that she planned to buy. Ideas for decorations, and things that she wanted to get done every day.

It seemed like more and more her to-do lists went undone.

He looked at her, and she looked just as good as she usually did, except...was it his imagination that she seemed a little bit paler than usual?

They went around the table, talking about dates that suited everyone and finally settling on something.

Roland didn't have to worry too much about it. All he had were the same things that everyone else had. He would be going to his nieces and nephews' programs and the church programs and... He didn't have a family of his own to worry about whether or not he would be here or there.

He supposed that was a positive, and he should appreciate that.

"Remember how we all used to sit around the fireplace on Christmas Eve and sing?" Amy asked, sitting beside Jones. Roland was pretty sure they had just had a kicking match underneath the table. But neither one of them seemed to be upset about it. It was just one of the things that Amy and Jones constantly did—they'd known each other forever.

"Those are some of my favorite memories. After we got home from the candlelight service at church, no one ever wanted to go to bed."

"I did," Marjorie said, raising her hand.

Everyone at the table laughed.

"Right, Mom. Everyone but you wanted to stay up."

"That's because Mom had to take all the gifts and put them around the tree."

"That's true. I always did that after you guys went to bed. I guess that's why I was always so tired on Christmas."

"I know. The Christmas afternoon nap is another great tradition we always used to have—one that I didn't appreciate until I was older," Wilson said with a laugh.

"I don't know why you waited until Christmas Eve to put the

gifts around the tree. It's not like you tried to convince us that Santa Claus was real or anything," Amy said.

"I didn't want you guys picking up the boxes and shaking them and figuring out what I had gotten you before we even got to Christmas," Marjorie said, like it was obvious.

"If you had kids, you'd know that," Isadora called from the other end of the table.

They all laughed, although there was a bit of sadness on Isadora's face that bothered Roland.

Still, he couldn't expect that a person would lose their husband and have their family be broken up and not have scars to show for it.

Later that evening, after the discussion at the table had ended, Roland found himself sitting on the floor in the living room, working on some props for the school play, and listening to the kids talk about their school and what they were doing.

Robert caught his ear when he talked about Miss Bushnell and the lines he was memorizing for their classroom play.

He knew exactly who Miss Bushnell was, and again, he tried to stop his sneer that automatically came when he heard her name.

It was an instinctive thing. Though Robert thought that she was a great teacher.

"We're really blessed to have Miss Bushnell as his teacher," Gilbert leaned over and said to Roland and Marjorie, who was sitting in the chair behind him.

"I know," Marjorie said with her voice low. "The other third grade teacher is a good teacher. Above average even. But Miss Bushnell is just absolutely extraordinary. She turns school into an experience that can't be replicated."

His mother would know. She'd been a teacher herself, homeschooling them at times when they were growing up. Plus, she had enough grandkids in school to know a good teacher when she saw one.

It felt odd, listening to his family go on about Miss Bushnell and all of her charms as Summer joined the conversation, speaking low so that the kids wouldn't hear. The adults certainly didn't want them to think any less of the other teacher, just in case the kids coming up didn't have Miss Bushnell. Although, they would certainly ask for her, which is what Summer said.

Roland figured that he ought to learn to at least have a tolerance for Nelly, since he probably was going to be hearing a lot about her over the years, because his siblings were almost certainly not done having children.

Unless he moved away, which he had absolutely no intention of doing. Who would take care of his mother? Who would run the Christmas tree farm? Who would be the Secret Saint?

He had really enjoyed the bit that he'd done and couldn't wait to get into more.

Later, before he left, he approached Wilson. "Have you noticed Mom?" he said as he zipped up his coat.

"What about her?" Wilson asked as he held up a coat for his wife.

"She just seems extra tired, doesn't she? Have you noticed anything?" He wanted to go on about the tiredness in her eyes and the fatigue that he'd seen, but he didn't want to put words in Wilson's mouth.

Wilson looked up to where his mother was deep in discussion with Amy and Terry.

"She looks fine to me," he said with a shoulder shrug.

Roland sighed and closed his mouth tight. It was frustrating that Wilson wouldn't at least give some credence to his words and look a little closer.

But he supposed he was in a hurry to get his wife and kids home and put them to bed.

Maybe Roland should have brought that up earlier in the evening.

But he knew as the baby of the family, he was the least likely to be taken seriously, even though he lived with his mom and saw her every day. It was hard to outgrow the "baby status" of being the youngest. Everyone treated him like he was still a kid, instead of a thirty-year-old adult.

"It was crazy. Somehow someone knew that we needed a special kind of dog food for the newest addition to our rescue, and that exact kind showed up the next morning—fifty pounds of it." Amy was speaking in hushed tones to Summer, and Roland stopped to listen.

"Do you think it's a Secret Saint thing?" Summer asked, sounding intrigued.

"I can't imagine who else it would be. I mean, that stuff is expensive. We had known that we were going to need it and were organizing a fundraiser just to buy that particular brand, but... someone heard about it, somehow, and dropped it off."

"I thought you had cameras up. Did they catch it?"

"We did. But the person was careful to park out of sight of the cameras, and they carried the dog food inside this cape thing. The hood was down low, and you really couldn't even tell whether it was a man or a woman because the cape hid the entire figure."

"Wow. That's really sweet. And I guess... It doesn't really matter if we ever find out who it is, does it?"

So...he had competition?

Wow. Whoever it was was organized and thoughtful. Roland had to admit some respect for this person who was apparently trying to usurp his position as the Secret Saint. He had been bequeathed as the next Secret Saint by Judd himself. This person was stepping on his toes but in a good way. It was nice that his family was being helped, since he probably wouldn't think to use his Secret Saint position to help anyone in his family. Although, Amy and Jones sometimes did struggle for money, because their shelter bills could become overwhelming. Jones, as a licensed veterinarian, could make a lot of money, but that didn't negate the fact that it still cost a lot to take care of the shelter animals, even though Jones could donate his own time and skills for a lot of things that other shelters would have to pay for or depend on donations for.

"I heard the Johnson family has a huge bill to pay from the car accident they had last summer, and they're not sure how they're going to buy heating fuel or firewood," Summer said. "I'm curious to see if the Secret Saint is going to donate any. I sure wish I knew who it was, because I don't have any firewood, but I would donate money in order for them to purchase some."

"It's fun to think of someone doing things anonymously, isn't it?" Charity said, nodding.

It sure was. Roland had to agree with that. He pretended to pull on his other boot while he continued to listen to their conversation talking about the Johnsons. He was already planning a firewood delivery for that evening. He had prepared carefully to make sure that he avoided detection. He would wait until his mom had gone to bed for the evening, and he'd already had the load of firewood that he was going to take sitting at the Christmas tree farm lot out of sight behind a shed.

He looked forward to loading up his pickup and taking it there. But it was going to take several hours, and he wanted to be able to get started as soon as he possibly could. He was determined to beat whoever this other Secret Saint might be and fill that need first.

He was pretty sure he had the best connections, because there wasn't anyone else in Mistletoe Meadows who had the family he did.

Sometimes it was a bit of a pain to have so many older siblings, and then sometimes, like now, it was a blessing.

He tightened the tie on his boot, pulled his pant leg down, and slowly stood.

"Thanks for the meal," he said to Summer and Gilbert as they helped his mom into her coat.

"It's always nice of you to come. I know you're single, and you could probably find a lot of other better things to do on a Friday night, but it's nice to have you show up."

"Oh, I don't know that there are too many better things to do than spend the evening with family. And the kids are cute. That helps."

"Don't you let him fool you. It's the food that brings him every time," Gilbert said with a smirk.

Roland lifted his shoulder. In times past, that probably would have been true. But now it was more like the family gossip brought him.

He laughed a little to himself, because it wasn't true. He loved his family and would always appreciate getting to spend time with them. But the gossip was definitely a perk right now.

He took his mom's arm, and they started out the door. He helped her into the car, and she gave a sigh of relief, her shoulders slumping, her head falling back against the headrest.

He walked around his truck thoughtfully.

After starting his pickup and moving out onto the road, knowing it was a short ride home, he didn't wait very long before he said, "Mom?"

"Hmm?" she said, her head still back and her eyes closed.

"Have you been feeling okay? I mean, is there something that you want to talk about regarding your health?"

That felt really odd coming out, especially toward his mom, but he didn't know how else to say it. He thought there was something going on, and short of saying, "I think you need to see a doctor," he didn't know how to phrase it.

"My goodness, no. I'm just fine. Why?" his mom said, lifting her head, opening her eyes, and putting a fake cheerful smile on.

He knew that smile. It was the kind of smile that she put on her face after getting six kids ready for church and fighting every one of them when they didn't want to get up on Sunday morning.

She didn't have to wear that smile too often, but he definitely recognized it.

"Mom. Are you feeling okay?"

"I'm feeling fine. But sometimes I do worry a little bit about you. I mean, I love that you're living with me, and I wouldn't trade that for the world, but I hope you're not here just because you think I need you."

"No. But I do think you need me."

"I do. But I wouldn't want you to stay with me and not do what you feel like God wants you to do with your life because you're too busy staying with me. You know?"

"Don't worry. If God wants me to move, I'm sure that He will show me, and I'm not going to say no to Him."

He paused and then tried another tack. "But since I'm living with you, and I see you every day, I feel like maybe you're not facing the fact that there might be something wrong with you?"

"I told you, I'm fine. There's nothing wrong. You worry too much. I think we ought to see about setting you up on a blind date. That's what I think. I suppose that would give me more energy than anything."

"Maybe not?" he said.

Marjorie laughed at his horrified reply, and then she launched into a story about a blind date that one of her classmates had set up for her in high school. It was a story he hadn't heard before, and he listened with interest. She effectively took his mind off his worry about her and her health and entertained him the rest of the way home. It wasn't until later that he realized that he hadn't gotten her to agree to go to the doctor like he wanted to.

Chapter Five

"Hello, darling. How was school today?" Grandma asked as Nelly arrived home, closing the door behind her and setting her bag down by the chair.

She had more work than usual, since she had spent her planning period discussing the school play with another teacher. She had what she was doing in her own classroom, plus the school play, but thankfully, the church had not tapped her for anything this year.

Although, things seemed to be running behind a little bit and maybe no one was planning on doing anything.

There was a part of her that wanted to jump in and make sure something was being planned, and if not, plan it herself, but she already had a lot of irons in the fire.

She thought about the firewood and smiled.

"Hello, Grandma. School was wonderful. The kids were great, and I think we all learned some things. Did you have a good day?"

"I did, but I cannot find my husband anywhere. He seems to have slipped away from me and did not let me know where he was going. I really don't like it when he does this. He knows I always want him to leave a note." Her grandmother looked very put out, although not worried.

Her words sent a squiggle of fear through Nelly's stomach. She had thought her gram was in her right mind today. She hadn't had an episode for over a week.

"I'm sure he'll be back soon, Gram. Would you like to go into the kitchen? I'm starving." She put an arm around her grandmother's shoulders and gently guided her toward the kitchen. It was funny, but being in the kitchen usually soothed her grandmother. Maybe it was because she had spent so much time there, creating delicious meals and dishes for her own family. Or maybe it was just being surrounded by the warmth and the good smells and the idea of sitting at the family table and laughing and talking with each other.

Whatever it was, Grandma always settled when they entered the room.

This time was no different.

"I sure hope those children didn't give you too much trouble today," her grandmother said, like the episode about her husband had never happened. She seemed to be back in the present.

"They didn't. They're good kids. I really love my class this year."

"You say that every year," Grandma teased her. And it was true. She always did think the class that she had currently was the best class she'd ever had. And she'd only been teaching for eight years. Was that the way it would always be?

"That's true. I guess I just always see their potential, you know?" she said, feeling the strain between her shoulder blades and flexing a bit to try to alleviate the pain. She had a long evening ahead of her before she could go to bed.

"That's one of the things I love about you. You were always so driven and competitive in school, and you still are, but you have such a big heart."

"Driven and competitive?" she said, although she knew it was true.

"Well, yes, you and that...McBride boy. Roland. The youngest. My goodness, you guys had such a competition going on."

"That's because he was mean to me, and I always wanted to outdo him."

"Yes, that's probably true. But you guys pushed each other to excellence. It was competition in the very best way. One year, you would win the spelling bee, then next year, he would."

"No. I won every year except for one, and that's when Jamie won." Jamie had ended up being the valedictorian of the class. It was funny, because she didn't remember any competition between her and Jamie, even though she had graduated number two. But she remembered tons of competition between her and Roland, and Roland hadn't even graduated in the top five. Their class had been small, and Roland had ranked well, but...not even next to her. It's funny—she remembered him as her main competitor.

"Every teacher you had commented on your rivalry with him. And how it was too bad that the two of you didn't get along, because instead of tearing each other down, your rivalry built each other up."

"I think that's true. I don't think I would have graduated number two in the class if it hadn't been for Roland. I was so determined to beat him at everything." She thought about other academic competitions, even any time they took a test. She didn't care who got the best grade in the class, whether it was her or someone else. She only cared that she beat Roland. Somehow, someway, she always found out his grade. Thankfully, she had a friend who sat behind him in almost every class, at least the ones where they were seated in alphabetical order according to last names. So she kind of had an inside scoop on what he made.

Somehow, he figured out how she did as well. It couldn't have been the person behind her, because that had been Jamie, and they had been friends.

Maybe it was someone who usually sat catty-corner from her. She wasn't sure, but...most of the memories were good. Even if her feelings about Roland were irritation more than anything.

"I always thought the two of you would end up together," Gram said as Nelly opened the refrigerator door and pulled out the salad fixings she had ready to put together for the meal.

"Roland and me?" she asked, aghast at the idea.

"Well, sure. You guys weren't competitive because you hated each other. You were competitive because you were attracted to each other."

Whoa. Was that true?

She didn't recall having tender feelings toward Roland. Not even one.

Did she?

She'd been so busy competing with him that she'd never stopped to examine how she might really feel. It was just so satisfying to beat him every time. She would think about the valentine that he had made fun of her about, the way she had cried and how hurt she'd been, and it just felt like that much more satisfaction.

"I do remember that teachers commented on our rivalry, and looking back, I think you're right. Roland made me a better student. He kept me focused on the things that I really should have been focused on, even if I wasn't doing them for exactly the right reasons."

"I think you're missing the point. There was some romantic interest between the two of you."

"I don't think there was," she said honestly. But in hindsight, maybe her grandmother was right. It was funny how she totally didn't notice anyone else or even care about their grades. She didn't even care about hers. As long as she beat Roland. She really hadn't thought of him in a romantic way, but maybe it was something that was there, just not on her radar.

She hadn't been interested in any other boys. And come to think of it, the ones she had gone out with hadn't consumed her the way Roland had. And maybe, just maybe, she had compared some of them to him and found them wanting.

"Now that you say something, maybe...maybe there was a bit of attraction there. I know I really enjoyed our rivalry, although I would have said that the thought of him turned my stomach and that he was mean and unkind and a big jerk. But...he really wasn't, was he?"

Her grandma smiled, kindly, as she chopped tomatoes at the table. She shook her head. "No. He really wasn't. He was a nice young man, and I was disappointed when the two of you didn't get together. I thought you were perfect for each other. The same way my Stuart was perfect for me. He was such a good man. Gone too soon."

Her grandma was quiet for a few beats, and Nelly had to admit that she was relieved that her gram seemed to be completely back in the present. The episodes of her being confused, or lost in the past, were scary and unsettling. She knew it was a part of growing older, and something that she had to face, but she didn't want to.

"So, anything new in town?" her gram asked.

One of the things that her gram really loved was the fact that Nelly still got out and told her all of the things that were going on. Her gram had different places that she went, and then they compared notes. It made her gram feel like she could still stay involved and made her less sad that she couldn't do all the things that she used to do.

"Well, I heard that the Johnson family needs firewood, and that came from the school nurse, who talked to one of the children, who had come to school and refused to take their coat off. Apparently, they were afraid that the school was going to be as cold as their house." She had felt bad for the little one and had determined to get the wood to the Johnson family as quickly as she could.

"Oh, that's sad. I remember cutting wood when I was young. I enjoyed doing that with my dad. He would take us all out into the woods with his chainsaw, cut up the logs into billets, and we would carry them to his pickup. It was work that my siblings really didn't enjoy, but I loved being out in the woods."

"I'm sure that was fun," Nelly said. She hadn't exactly gone out in the woods and gotten hers. She had strategically talked to someone who knew someone who owned a log truck. That person had brought her a load of firewood, paid for in cash by someone who knew someone. Then, she paid someone else to cut it up.

She was going to go herself in Gram's old pickup, which of course used to be her grandpa's, and take a load to the Johnson family.

She'd been setting it up for a while, because she'd heard that they had a bill and couldn't afford their heat and had turned their heat way down so they didn't have to order oil before Christmas. Hearing about the little one who refused to take his coat off had made her step up her efforts, and she was ready to do it tonight.

She had her eye on midnight or slightly thereafter. She figured she could take a little nap before she left and then sleep a bit afterward. That seemed to be the best time, and then that gave her four hours give or take to load her pickup and then unload it at the Johnsons'. She might even be able to get two loads if she hurried.

She wasn't sure exactly how long it would take, but it felt good to be planning it and to know that tomorrow morning, the Johnsons' worry about keeping their house warm would be completely over.

Chapter Six

Roland arrived at the Johnsons' about a half an hour after midnight. He parked down the street, even though it would mean slipping through the Johnsons' backyard and a little bit of extra walking. It was worth it in order not to meet anyone. He didn't want to lose his anonymity, especially not this early in the year. Judd was counting on him, but he had his own personal goals as well—he was really enjoying the Secret Saint thing. It made him feel like he had a purpose, and it made him feel happy and good inside to do good for others. He didn't want to lose that.

There was something about no one knowing who he was that made it extra special.

If everyone knew he was doing it, it just wouldn't be as fun. The idea of sneaking around and making it happen without people finding out was just too delicious and really worked with his goofy and somewhat silly personality.

He supposed that was the way the youngest always was—a little bit of a baby at times. Although he hated to admit it and wished he could shake that reputation.

Regardless, he parked the truck, grabbed an armful of wood, and started toward the Johnson house.

Their woodpile was off to the side in the front by their outdoor furnace. He stacked the first load of wood and turned to walk back toward his truck, adjusting his ski mask to make sure that it completely covered his face.

He'd even bought different boots than what he normally wore for his Secret Saint gig.

These were driving boots—they had good traction but no ties. He really enjoyed the way they felt on his feet and had been tempted to wear them more often even when he wasn't in his Secret Saint getup.

No sooner had he thought that than a figure came from out of the blue. He saw it a second before it ran right into him and wood scattered everywhere.

"Umph!" a voice said, and his voice echoed that as he tripped on a piece of wood that had fallen and landed on his butt, his hands behind him, facing the figure who was also on the ground—the one that had knocked him down.

"I'm sorry," a quiet voice came out of the dark. It was low, but... he couldn't quite tell if it was a man or a woman.

"No. It was my fault. I was thinking about something and wasn't paying attention," he said.

The figure moved, starting to pick up the firewood.

It was dawning on him...was this person also delivering firewood for the Johnson family?

He didn't recognize the voice, but he wanted to see if he could get them to talk so that maybe he could. On that note, he started gathering up some of the wood around him.

"Excuse me," he said, reaching across the person, just hoping that they would speak.

"No. Excuse me," the person said, and then he realized they were reaching for the same piece of firewood, picking it up together, each of them holding onto an end as they both tried to look into each other's eyes.

But he couldn't see anything. The person had a cape or cloak on with a deep hood that completely covered their face. They were wearing gloves, so he couldn't see anything about their hands, other than they were smaller than his, but were they the size of a woman's hands? Or just a man who was smaller?

He couldn't tell whether the body was thin or fat or something in between. The cloak hid everything.

"I'm sorry," the voice said again, and this time, it sounded like a little bit of humor laced the words.

He could see something funny in this. It was kind of odd that the two of them were delivering firewood, had run into each other, and now they were reaching for the same piece.

"No. I apologize," he said, making sure to mask his voice as it seemed like the other person was. He hardly thought that someone would wonder whether he was a man or a woman, but he whispered, trying to make it less obvious.

Who could it be? He ran through all the people that he knew in town. As they stood, with the other person letting go of the firewood, allowing him to take it, he realized they were much smaller than he was.

A woman? Or just a short man?

"Please don't tell anyone you saw me," the other person said.

"I won't if you won't," Roland said.

The person continued to the woodpile, and he stacked his one piece and then waited.

Without saying anything, the person turned, and they walked back to the back of the house together. Through the darkness, through the yard, slowly and silently. He was very aware of the person beside him, but they didn't talk.

He realized that the person might not realize that he was bringing firewood too.

Should he pretend to not be? Or should he go to his truck and grab an armful, and let them know that he was in on this too?

"It seems like we both have the same idea," he finally said, once they were past the Johnsons' house.

"You're delivering firewood too?" the careful reply came.

"Yeah. I heard they needed it."

"Same."

There was quiet for a moment.

"If I get done first, I'll help you with yours."

"Cool," came the cautious reply. He realized that maybe whoever it was wouldn't want him to see their vehicle—maybe he would recognize it.

He didn't think anyone would recognize his. It was an old truck that they used on the farm. Typically it didn't go off the farm, because it wasn't inspected. It was just an old farm truck.

But he supposed anyone who had been on the tree farm might have an idea that someone in the McBride family could possibly be the Secret Saint. That's probably the only conclusion they would come to. He decided not to worry about it, because the odds that they would recognize it were highly unlikely.

They didn't say anything else but separated when they were almost to the street, the other person having parked up the street, while he parked down.

They met again, both of them carrying an armful of wood.

"It's a nice night for a Secret Saint to be out," he said.

"That's what I was thinking," came that ironic reply. "And that would be...you or me?"

There was humor in the words again that struck Roland. Was it familiar? He wasn't sure.

He was pretty sure it was a woman though. There was a husky note there that he found...attractive? He wasn't sure.

He couldn't be attracted to someone he couldn't see, right?

Still, as they walked side by side through the side yard, questions kept popping into his head.

"I've heard a couple of other people might need help. Maybe we should compare notes and team up." There. It was a bit of relief to actually say it. After all, there was a part of him that wanted to be competitive, that was a little bit annoyed that this person was finding the same people that he was and doing kind things for them. But...why not? He would much rather work together than work against someone.

He thought about high school and the competition between Nelly and him.

Nelly had always taken it a lot more seriously than he had, and most of the time, he only tried to beat her just to see how frustrated and angry she got when he won. It was funny to watch, but he didn't really enjoy winning. He enjoyed much more the feeling of camaraderie when two people worked together. Maybe that was because he came from such a big family, where his siblings and he were always doing things together, and he loved to be included, especially since he was the youngest and often was too young for the things that they were doing. He hated feeling left out, so working together was something that he always strove for.

One wouldn't think it to remember the heated competition between Nelly and him all through high school. And even before that. It probably started about the time of that stupid valentine. He wished he would never have said anything. It had made her mad in such a way that she'd never forgotten it. He was pretty sure that was why she always felt like she needed to one-up him.

He didn't hate her, but...their competition had been kind of fun in a way. Still, he'd rather work together.

"I don't know," the person said, stacking wood alongside him.

They walked back and forth, the work seeming to be a lot easier and go faster now that he was with someone. He liked it.

They chatted softly each time they were past the Johnsons' house about different people that they knew who needed help, and he really could see the benefits of them working together.

"This is my last load. Do you still have more?" he asked after they had made what felt like a hundred trips back and forth between their pickups and the woodshed.

"I just have a little bit more," the person said.

"Do you mind if I give you a hand?"

They went and stacked their current load together until they were finished. The person put the last piece of wood on the huge stack that had appeared in the Johnsons' yard overnight and put their hands on their hips—at least it looked that way from the way their cloak moved and jutted out at the sides.

"How do I know I can trust you?"

"You could rat me out the same as I could do to you."

"You might recognize my vehicle."

"You might recognize mine," he said, although he really wasn't concerned about that.

"I don't know. I really enjoy doing this anonymously, and I don't want anyone to find out who I am."

"I'm exactly the same. There's just a certain satisfaction in doing things that people don't know that you're doing. And...you just do it for the fun of helping someone, not for the accolades that come along with it. You know?"

"Exactly. There's just such a deep sense of satisfaction, and I don't want to lose that."

"Me either. Tell you what, I know you don't have any reason to think that I would keep my word, but let's shake on it. I promise that I will not try to find out your identity, and if by accident I do, it will go no further than me."

The person looked at him for a bit. He could almost feel their thoughtful stare from the depths of their cloak before they finally nodded their head.

"I guess that's the best it's going to get." They sighed. "I promise the same. That I will not try to find out your identity, and if I do accidentally figure it out, I will not tell a soul."

They looked at each other, nodded, and then their gloved hands clasped, and they shook.

Normally, he would have taken his glove off, but just in case the person was still wondering whether they were dealing with a man or a woman, or just in case there was some kind of identifying mark on his hand that he didn't know about, he kept his glove on.

They did the same. And that was it—a camaraderie, a partnership had been born.

He went to their truck and helped with the last of the wood as they chatted together.

He wasn't sure whether they had agreed to help each other or just not to tell on each other.

As they finished up, he wasn't sure how to broach the subject. They talked about other people who needed help and carefully discussed things—carefully as in he tried not to say anything that would give away any of his sources or any of the identities of anyone that he talked to. In other words, he couldn't mention that he had heard this at a family gathering. He had to skirt around the truth, which did not sit well with him.

She, he was pretty sure it was a she, seemed to be equally careful and equally uncomfortable.

As they walked back away after stacking the last bit of wood, they turned together, almost as if they had decided to, and stood looking at the night's work. It was a nice, large stack of wood that would definitely see the family through December, although he had plans to bring more.

But the person with him didn't say anything more about their plans, and he didn't want to tip his hand either.

"All right, I guess that was a pretty good night."

"I guess so," she said as the two of them turned around, walking together through the yard one last time.

He was kind of surprised how well they had worked together. And how at ease he had felt, and he had a grudging respect for their planning and execution. He ought to know that it wasn't easy to anonymously get an entire load of firewood and somehow arrive at someone's house at midnight without anyone else knowing. He assumed that the other person had just as much crafty manipulation as he had. He grudgingly admired them.

"Well, it was good to meet you, I guess."

"Same," the person said, their head seeming to tilt under the cloak. "I guess...this is goodbye."

"I suppose it is."

He wanted to say something, but...he wasn't sure how they felt and didn't want to propose something only to be left out in the cold.

"I'd say try to be more careful and not run into anyone in the middle of the night."

"I'd say the same thing to you."

They laughed a little, and then the other person put up their arm, and the cloak fell back a bit.

That slender arm could almost only belong to a woman.

But the wave was a quick one, and he didn't have time to dwell on it.

"Be safe," the other person said.

"Same to you," he said, and after another last glance at each other, they both turned and walked away.

Who could that be?

Chapter Seven

*N*elly clutched the coffee in her hand and tried to stay awake while she went around the classroom, each student giving their homework answer.

They had switched papers and were correcting them in class.

Nelly didn't do that often, but she was exhausted today and wasn't sure whether or not she would be able to correct anything after school tonight. Especially with the emergency churchwide meeting that had been called. Apparently, someone had realized there was no Christmas play scheduled for this year.

Nelly desperately wanted to be involved in that, and she wanted to pretend that she wasn't so tired that she was struggling to stay awake.

"Miss Bushnell?" one of the students closest to her desk whispered to her.

She realized that the classroom had been quiet for a while.

"I'm sorry," she said, lifting the coffee to her lips and taking another sip. It was almost time to go home—she would be wired until midnight. Or...the way she felt, she would be hard-pressed to go to the meeting without taking a nap first.

She looked around the classroom. "Everyone, figure out how many questions the person you corrected missed and then give them their paper back."

She continued on with math class, embarrassed that a student had noticed her inattention. She prided herself on keeping her personal feelings completely separate from anything that had to do with school.

She had to remember that just a few moments later, when Roland McBride arrived to collect Robert from her classroom.

She pasted a smile on her face and remembered that Robert had given her an excuse to leave slightly early for a dentist appointment.

Apparently his uncle was taking him to the dentist appointment.

She could be nice, she could be kind, she could interact with this person that she intensely disliked.

She walked over, as she would with any other parent, and greeted him. "Good afternoon. Robert will be ready in just a moment. We were just a bit late with math class today, and we're running slightly over. Let him get his things gathered up and put in his book bag."

"Sure. We'll just be late for the dentist, that's all," Roland said, sounding casual, but his words were anything but. It was a passive-aggressive swipe at her, saying that she wasn't a good teacher, and she was going to cause them to be late.

"I said I was sorry," she said, using her best professional teacher's voice and her best professional teacher's smile. The kind of smile that she would smile at parents that she knew weren't doing the best things that they possibly could for their children but were instead handing them off to the school to babysit every day. And who didn't really give a flip whether their children learned anything or not. Those were her least favorite kind of parents.

Probably it was her physical exhaustion that caused her to work even harder at being cool and collected.

"You always did have trouble being on time," Roland said. "But at least you got the right student."

It was a dig at the fact that she had given her valentine to the wrong person. Actually, it really hadn't been her fault. The only thing she could ever figure out was that she had put Tommy's valentine in Roland's envelope, but she never could confirm it. She had been too shy to go to Tommy and ask if he had gotten a valentine from her.

She had given Roland one that basically said "you stink, but have a happy Valentine's Day anyway."

It was the nastiest one she could find, which was saying something, because most of the valentines were pretty nice and benign.

"I guess some people just hold onto the past and can't ever let it go, can they?" she said, her smile not slipping an inch.

"Boy, that's someone to talk—someone who had a rivalry over a valentine the entire way from third grade to twelfth."

"I don't know what you're talking about," she said, lifting her chin and giving him a superior look.

"I'm talking about the fact that you had your friend spy on me so that you knew every single grade that I got and made sure that yours were higher. That's what I'm talking about."

Nelly was aware of her students and their curiosity about the visitor and their conversation even though they were supposed to be practicing their handwriting.

"That is an unfair accusation, Mr. McBride. But you're used to being wrong, aren't you?"

"I doubt I'm used to it as much as you are, Miss Bushnell. But wrong, late, whatever."

She didn't get to say anything more, because Roland said, "Hey, Robert. Glad you got your stuff gathered together. I'm here to rescue you."

"We like to encourage our children to enjoy school and not use such language that would make them think that there was something wrong with being here."

"I'd do that too, but I don't like to lie to kids," Roland said.

She wanted to stamp her foot in frustration. She really, really loved Robert, and he had so much potential. Roland was going to ruin it all because of some stupid competition.

But even as she thought that, she knew the competition was all her fault.

She lifted her chin as Roland turned his back, put his hand on Robert's shoulder, and walked him out the door.

She truly wanted the best for the children, and if she had to bite her tongue and smile at Roland in order to do it, she would.

"I'm sorry, children, let's make sure we're doing the best we can as we practice our cursive Zs."

She arrived at home later that afternoon, and thankfully, Grandma was having a good day. She had been talking to her colleagues about how long she should try to keep her grandmother at home and what her options were. She couldn't stay home from school and watch her every day, and she wasn't sure she could hire someone to stay there all day long. But she didn't want to send her grandma to a home if she could help it. The idea made her sad and also made her feel like she wasn't being a very good granddaughter.

Regardless, she and Gram had a good meal together, and she even caught a nap before she headed to the meeting.

Marjorie McBride was there, and while she knew that Marjorie was Roland's mother, she loved the woman completely and sometimes had trouble believing that the two of them could be related.

She was greeted by her and several other people as they walked in.

Pastor Connelly apologized for the short notice and explained that that was why a lot of people couldn't make it.

"But I felt like we had to take care of the situation immediately. I'm sorry that I've been distracted by my wife's illness and haven't been on this like I should. I was hoping, Nelly, that you would volunteer to head it up. I know you're very busy with your school and classroom, but no one does the job the way you do."

"Yes. Absolutely. I'd love to do it," Nelly said honestly. She really did love working on the school play and figured that she could probably fit that into her schedule. Although, it was going to be an intense four weeks of practice, since the church play usually was done the Sunday after Christmas.

"That's wonderful. My son, Roland, told me on my way out that he would be able to help as well. He was going to be a little late to the meeting, but he wanted me to volunteer him, because he had to take his nephew to the dentist, and he had just gotten home as I was walking out."

Nelly about swallowed her tongue when Marjorie started to talk. She would be having to work with Roland? She could hardly take her volunteering back. That would be very un-Christian of her.

"I see. Well, it looks like we have our two directors lined up. Now, let's talk about dates and refreshments."

She realized that what was in her heart wasn't what was coming out in her actions. Her heart was black and wicked and didn't want to have anything to do with Roland. But here she was, pretending there were no problems. She needed to fix her heart, not back out of working with Roland.

The meeting was almost ready to wrap up when she noticed that Roland slipped in the back door and sat down beside his mom.

His mom leaned over and whispered to him, and Nelly almost laughed out loud at the expression on Roland's face.

She looked away quickly as his eyes started to lift—she was sure that he would be searching the crowd looking for her.

Pastor Connelly noticed his late arrival and announced from where he stood at the front, "Looks like Roland has arrived. Just want to let you know that your mom volunteered you, and you are now working with Nelly Bushnell to direct the play. We've been talking about budget constraints, and the expectations of the play, and also the fact that we're going to have to have some extra practices during the week. I hope that will work with your schedule?"

"This is a busy time of year at the Christmas tree farm," Roland began, almost as though he were going to try to gracefully back out of it, but then—she didn't know whether he remembered that he had told his mom he would do it, or whether she pinched him where no one could see, but he pasted an obviously fake smile on his face and said, "but I'm happy to help out wherever I can. That's what I told my mom when she left, and whatever she volunteered me for, I'll keep my word and honor her commitment."

Nelly wanted to put her arms over her chest and pout. She didn't want to work with Roland. And she didn't want to have to explain why. Because she couldn't. She really had no idea.

The rest of the meeting passed without her paying a whole lot of attention. It would be up to her and Roland to set the practice schedule and figure out exactly what they were going to do. That meant she was going to have to talk to him after the meeting adjourned.

She wasn't looking forward to it, and she wanted him to come to her.

Except she didn't. She wanted to be the one in control. So, as soon as Pastor Connelly closed the meeting with prayer, she jumped up and went marching over to Roland. Halfway over, she realized she was acting like she was going on a death march, and she tried to modulate her speed and her directness.

She paused to give Mrs. Tucker a polite smile. That soon turned sour when Mrs. Tucker said, "I'm thrilled that the two of you are working together. I always thought that the two of you in high school were just absolutely brilliant. You motivated each other to do far, far better than either one of you would have done by yourselves. Of course, my Jamie was valedictorian, but I had to admire how you and Roland just were so determined to push each other to be your very, very best."

Nelly practically bit her tongue in order to not respond to Mrs. Tucker the way she wanted to.

She heard snickering and turned in time to see Roland tucking a laugh back behind his hands.

It made her mad again, and it was all she could do to keep her eyes from flashing as she wanted to fly over to him and grab him by his ears.

Instead, she politely thanked Mrs. Tucker, complimented the woman on the Christmas cookies that she always provided for the after-show refreshments, and told her she was looking forward to the treats again this year. Then, she politely excused herself because she had a few details to hash out with Mr. McBride. She emphasized the "Mr." as she turned and strode toward Roland, who hadn't budged from his mother's side. As though he needed to hide behind his mother's skirts for protection.

Which, come to think of it, maybe he did.

"Mr. McBride. It looks like you and I are going to be working together." She wanted to add, "and you can't be any happier about that than I am, so let's make the best of it," but there were people within earshot, so she just gave him a fake smile.

She felt the wickedness of her heart down to her soul and wished there was something that she could do to make herself actually be nice. After all, Roland wasn't the devil.

Just the closest thing she knew to it.

"Looks like it," Roland said, shoving his hands in his pockets and smirking at her. "I guess I'll just let you do what you do best, which is boss everyone around, and I'll do whatever you tell me to do. Which will be the safest choice."

"That's not the way partnership works."

His brows raised. "Oh?" he said, as though he didn't know how partnerships were supposed to work.

"Yes. We're supposed to give our opinions and then talk it out."

"All right. What's your opinion on what program we should do?"

"Well, of course we need to do Mary and Joseph. That's the program that we always do."

"Yeah, we've done that over and over again. Let's do something different this year."

"Of course not. Not only are we going to do what the church has traditionally always done, but we don't have time to work up anything else." She felt her voice hitting screech level, and she toned it down. Or at least tried to.

"See? Like I said, I'll just do whatever you tell me to do."

"Well, you have to be reasonable. Of course, you can give your opinion, but you just can't change stuff that has never been changed."

"I wouldn't dream of it," he said.

Nelly felt herself wanting to back out, but she knew that the church relied on this outreach to bring in people, who might normally not be in church, to hear the gospel story. It brought kids in who might not go to church every Sunday but who came during the Christmas season. It was an important outreach of the church, and she didn't want to ruin it.

Plus, she was very aware of everyone watching them. Some of them were smiling, almost endearingly, like they remembered their high school rivalry and thought it was cute.

Nelly didn't think it was cute. It was annoying, as annoying as the man in front of her was.

"I think it's important that we honor our tradition, but if you have any suggestions, you certainly are welcome to tell them to me."

"I already did. You shut me down. Let's just figure out the practice schedule."

She gritted her teeth. She wanted to argue with him—actually no, she wanted to grab him by the throat and smack his head against the wall, but his mother was standing right there, so she thought she probably ought to restrain herself. Although, the poor woman must be a saint and surely knew what it was like to want to grab a hold of Roland.

Be nice. Just be nice.

She had to remind herself that she was a Christian, and she was supposed to love people. Especially those who were of the household of faith. That included, allegedly, Roland.

Interesting how he brought out her absolute worst side.

After all, she was exceptionally interested in getting children into the church, along with their families, so that they could hear the good news of the gospel. Unfortunately, if she continued to spar with Roland, she would not be a very good example of how the gospel could change a person's life.

It really had changed hers, just…sometimes she allowed her flesh to take over. Like anytime Roland was around.

Hopefully, her love for the children and her genuine desire to see Jesus be glorified would overcome these fleshly instincts to be unkind and mean to someone who really, probably didn't deserve it, if she was being honest.

"All right," she said in a calm tone. "I think we should practice every day of the week and have an extra long practice on Saturdays. I'm sure if we put it to the church, someone will volunteer to make food for us, and we can break on Saturdays to eat and then go back to practicing. If we have that much time, I'm sure we can pull it together beautifully."

"You want to practice every single day and hours and hours on Saturday? There's no need for that. We're just doing the Mary and Joseph thing. Everybody knows how it goes. There are no surprises, and it doesn't take that much practice."

She almost smiled, because it sounded like he was irritated. Almost, because she was as irritated as he was and did not feel like smiling. "We've got to get it right. This is an important part of the church ministry. People get saved because of this. People have their lives changed because of this program. We can't be relaxed about it." What did he not understand about that?

She realized she was getting heated again and could tell from her peripheral vision that people were looking at her.

"We're not being relaxed about it," he said, putting air quotes around the word. "We're just being reasonable. People have a lot of things to do this time of year. They don't have time to have intense practices over a church program that isn't that hard to learn. We don't have to have people giving up their entire Saturdays, cooking for us, and sacrificing time when they should be spending it together as a family during the Christmas season."

He sounded just as annoyed as she did. But again, she knew they weren't presenting a very good example for the people around them.

"All right. Fine. We can practice half as many times as what I originally proposed."

"Three times a week and two hours on Saturday?" he said, his eyes narrowed.

"If you feel that's sufficient. But I do want it to be known that if this is not a complete and total success, it is all your fault."

That seemed a little unreasonable, but at the same time, she would practice for hours upon hours, just to get every little detail right. He on the other hand was much more likely to wing it, counting on his natural talent and intelligence to get things right.

It was frustrating to her that all through their school years, he'd stayed close in competition with her, without putting in nearly the effort that she had. Maybe that was part of why he was so annoying to her.

But that seemed petty and small, and she definitely didn't want to think that about herself.

"They always did have this rivalry going on between them," someone said. It was a lady's voice, but Nelly didn't turn to look. Her tiredness had been forgotten, and all she wanted to do was win the argument with Roland.

"I know. Nelly always insisted on winning, but...sometimes I think Roland just let her win."

She almost turned and snapped at whoever had even insinuated that.

Even though she had just pretty much thought the exact same thing herself.

But she collected herself and tried to speak rationally to Roland.

"We can start—we can announce this on Sunday, recruit the kids, and start practices Monday. We'll have them Monday, Wednesday, Friday and for two hours on Saturday morning. Does that sound okay?"

He nodded. "That's fine. I'll help however I can."

He didn't look enthused about it at all—in fact, he looked like he couldn't wait to get away from her, which made two of them.

Why in the world would he have volunteered to do anything? Didn't he know that she always volunteered for this? She'd headed it up for the last eight years, ever since she'd gotten out of college. And before that, she'd directed it in high school too.

She even helped the person who had done it during her college years. It was ridiculous that he would even volunteer, unless he was secretly planning on sabotaging it?

She couldn't rule that out, although she didn't think Marjorie would be included in that kind of plan, and she didn't think that Roland would do something so sinister and break his mother's heart.

Still, without his mother there, she thought he was perfectly capable of it. Sadly.

She tried to push all of that out of her mind as she walked slowly home. More to get her mind off Roland than anything, she thought about the helper that she now had, or seemed to have anyway, for her Secret Saint activities.

Now, she would not mind trying to figure out who in the world it could be. Possibilities exploded through her mind, and she blissfully forgot, for just a few moments anyway, that she was going to have to work with Roland McBride for the next few weeks on the Christmas program. Ugh.

In fact, she thought, as she walked along, maybe she should initiate contact with the other Secret Saint. He seemed pretty interested in a partnership, and they had shaken on it that they would not reveal their identities. Plus, she had several things that she wanted to do, but she couldn't quite do by herself. Perhaps...

Perhaps a little camaraderie was in order. A pleasant camaraderie, unlike what she was going to have to deal with with the Christmas play.

The thought made her smile, and she began to plan out exactly how she could relay her message to someone she did not know the identity of. She thought she could figure it out.

Chapter Eight

*R*oland pulled a box of wrapping paper, bows, and ribbons out of his pickup and shut the door with his elbow.

He was careful not to slam it, careful not to make any more noise than absolutely necessary.

He had made a delivery a few days earlier to the Roberts family with groceries and a few items that he had found out were on the children's Christmas list. Then, from his sister Terry, he found out that they didn't have money to buy wrapping paper to wrap the gifts.

Hence, his second delivery tonight.

He was always hesitant to go to a house two nights very close to each other because if it were him, and he really wanted to know who the Secret Saint was, he would be keeping an eye out for someone to show up.

So, he was extra cautious.

But he did wonder whether he would meet the other Secret Saint tonight.

Wishing he could adjust his ski cap so that he was sure that it covered all of his face, he gripped the box and continued to walk, keeping an eye out. Would she be here?

She seemed to have some of the same channels that he did, or maybe they were different but just as good. He wasn't sure, but he knew that meeting her was not completely out of the question. It's why he had chosen this time—that was the time he had met her before, and she seemed to work the same time he did.

Still, there was no sign of her as he walked to the back porch and set his box down.

He was just about to straighten and go when his eyes caught on something white that stuck out from underneath the rug.

And that's when he realized there was a box on the other side of the porch with the same type of supplies—wrapping paper, bows and ribbons, name tags, anything a family might need to wrap presents up for their children.

He almost stood and laughed, but he remembered the need to be cautious.

And what was that white thing?

Should he just leave it? It might be for the Roberts family. But who kept a piece of paper under their back doormat?

Figuring that if it wasn't actually his, he could return it, he grabbed the paper, shoved it up his sleeve, and hurried off, looking in all directions, not just to make sure that he wasn't caught but also to see if the other Secret Saint was around. Had she waited on him? Would she want to talk?

Was the note from her?

He had to admit that's what he was hoping.

He didn't take the note out of his sleeve until he had made it home, parked his truck behind the shed on the tree farm, and got in the ATV that he used to drive from his mother's house to the farm.

It was back roads, and thankfully the ATV had a heater in the cab.

It also did not have a dome light, but he couldn't wait another minute to read the letter, so while he was waiting for the engine to warm, he grabbed his phone, flipped the flashlight on, and pulled the piece of paper out of his sleeve.

He had to laugh at himself a little, because he was going to be crushed if it wasn't from the other Secret Saint. He had really gotten his hopes up.

Anticipation swirled in his stomach as he opened the folded sheet.

In very neat, printed handwriting, there was a simple sentence.

Meet me at the gazebo tomorrow night at midnight. – SS

"Wow." Roland stared at the paper, reading the short message over again and letting it filter into his brain. She wanted to meet?

Did he want to do that? Would he?

He blinked and then stared off into space for a bit. Was this wise? Was someone just trying to unmask him? Or maybe they were trying to set him up for some kind of nefarious reason.

But he knew the other Secret Saint had been there—her box sat there on the porch. So...this could actually be real.

And what was the worst that could happen if it wasn't an actual Secret Saint, but just someone trying to set him up for something? What was the worst that could happen? He'd just lose the anonymity that he really loved.

But he wasn't doing anything wrong. It wasn't like someone was going to take him to prison or catch him at anything.

Tucking it in his pocket and putting the ATV in gear, he decided he would go home and sleep on it. Maybe he'd even run it by Judd if he saw him the next day. Although, it was going to be a busy day because the fire company in Whisker Hollow had run out of Christmas trees and thought they could sell another tractor-trailer load before Christmas, so starting at 6 AM, he was going to be cutting and wrapping Christmas trees in order to load them when the truck got there around noon.

Since it was just him, it was probably going to take all day, and there would be the occasional private shopper who stopped at the Christmas tree farm to buy their tree.

The closer they got to Christmas, the more shoppers who showed up randomly during the day. Of course, weekends were always the busiest.

Still, he had a full day in front of him, and he had a pretty big decision to make.

He had a little bit of trouble getting to sleep once he finally got in bed. Who was this mystery Secret Saint? Was it someone he knew? Was it an older woman? Was it someone his own age?

He had to admit that he hoped it was someone close to his age, because he felt...something when he was working with her. An attraction, a pull, a desire to know more about her, other than just blatant curiosity, which was to be expected, considering the anonymity of both of their identities.

Was he wise to have this growing investment in an anonymous relationship? Because, if he did decide to meet her, he was not going to let her know his identity. If that was what she wanted, it wasn't going to happen. He had to stand firm on that. He could be the Secret Saint for the next twenty or thirty or more years, if he was careful and didn't get himself into a situation where he had to reveal his identity.

He wasn't looking at this as a short-term thing—unless he got married and had a family and was no longer able to do it, he could do this for the rest of his life pretty much.

But again, it was up to him to be careful.

He had almost had himself talked out of accepting the invitation. It wasn't like he had to write her back or anything—he could wait until the very last minute to decide to go.

Maybe that's what he would do. He would go, but he would hang back until he saw whether or not she showed up at the gazebo. If it looked legit, if he felt okay about it, if he didn't see any reason why he shouldn't step into the open with his ski cap on and his jacket and boots that he wore only for Secret Saint activities, then he would step out too.

With that decision made, he rolled over, although it was still a long time before he fell asleep.

Chapter Nine

"Hi, Grandma," Nelly said as she walked in the door, setting her school bag down. She had papers to correct, but it was a fairly short quiz and shouldn't take her too long. She had been able to use her planning period to get caught up on everything else and get ready for tomorrow.

She had found herself having a little bit of trouble concentrating in class today. After all, she was nervous and excited, and a little bit scared. Would the Secret Saint accept her invitation?

And was that a wise invitation to issue?

She thought about how well they had worked together and how his skills seemed to complement hers. He had the big hands of a working man, and there were so many things that a Secret Saint could do, like fixing a porch, changing the oil in cars, and even putting on a new roof. Plus, he was much better at carrying firewood than she was, and he was probably better at getting it too.

She was better at groceries, gifts for kids, and organizing everything.

She really hoped that they could combine their skills, and

perhaps instead of one plus one equaling two, they could multiply what they could do.

She had thought long and hard about issuing the invitation and had finally decided that even though there were a lot of cons, the benefits would be astronomical if they turned out to be even a little bit of what she hoped they could be.

But there was the danger that he would try to unmask her. Even if he didn't physically try, he might ask her to pull her hood down so he could see, and she was determined that she would not do it. It was important that she keep her identity a secret. She didn't want anyone in her classroom thinking that she was playing favorites with any of her students if she did Secret Saint activities for some of her students and not for all of them. Some of them didn't need it. But that might not stop them from becoming offended or from accusing her of not being a fair teacher.

She didn't want it to affect her classroom at all. Those students were the most important thing in the world to her, after her grandmother.

"I had a wonderful day, Gram. How are you?" she asked, holding her breath a little because her grandma had had a lot of really good days, and Nelly was afraid that a bad day was coming.

"I'm fantastic. I heard you whistling this morning when you first got up. You always seem to be really happy after you've been out running around doing that stuff you've talked about."

She had often wished that she hadn't shared with her grandmother what she was doing, but because her gram kept such odd hours and was up often in the middle of the night, she had felt like it was something that she probably had to do.

But with her grandma's failing faculties, she was afraid that her grandma might accidentally let it slip. She knew, with an absolute certainty, that it was something her gram in her normal life would never have allowed to come out.

"Remember that you're not allowed to talk to anyone about

that," she said gently, putting an arm around her gram and giving her a hug.

"I know. It's called the Secret Saint because you want to keep it a secret." Her gram lifted a brow and spoke with humor. "But what you don't realize is back when I was growing up, there was a Secret Saint."

"There was?" Her gram was right—she hadn't realized.

"I wasn't very little. But maybe about the time I had my own children, we had one year where my husband was off work because he had the flu. Back then, we didn't get paid at all while he was off, after he used up all of his vacation. And I knew Christmas was going to be tight. But the Secret Saint came along and gave us an entire box of gifts that I could wrap up for my children. Somehow, they knew exactly what each kid wanted and had gotten everything on their list. I have no idea how they found out that information. I had only confided in a few people, and none of them were the Secret Saint, I was sure of it. They included a sweet note, and Christmas was really nice that year, because of someone's generosity."

"Was the note signed 'the Secret Saint'?"

"It was. But either we didn't talk about those things back then, or the Secret Saint didn't do much work, because I never heard of anyone else getting anything like that that year. Maybe they just did one thing every year, because after that, I did keep an eye out to see if anything happened to anyone else. The words 'Secret Saint' had glued themselves into my brain, and my ears would perk up if I even heard something that sounded similar."

"And did you?" Nelly asked, amazed that there was a history of the Secret Saint. She had never heard about this before.

"I did. About once a year—it wasn't even always at Christmas—I would hear something that happened to someone. And then, oh goodness, it must have been about twenty years after that—twenty years ago—when it stopped completely. I don't know if the person died or moved away, or if they just weren't in a position to be able to do that anymore."

"I would really love to know. But I wouldn't have the first idea of how to start going about trying to figure it out. I mean, who would you even ask? It happened to you, and you have no idea."

"No. The handwriting was printed, very carefully, like someone didn't want us to be able to recognize the writing. And everyone's note looked different. From what I remember, a few of them were typed. And they didn't always leave a note."

"Do you think it was a woman?" Nelly asked. She for some reason just thought it probably was a woman. Even though the person that she had left the note for last night—she knew that was a man. Knew it just the way she knew that the sun was in the sky, even though she couldn't see it. But it just seemed like the Secret Saint would be a woman's idea.

"I always thought it was a man. Sometimes the packages were pretty heavy, and I guess I just see men being able to sneak around in the middle of the night better than women anyway. It could be dangerous for a woman to be out in the middle of the night."

"Not in Mistletoe Meadows. It's totally safe here."

"True," Gram said. "Although you never know."

She supposed that was true. Bad things could happen to someone anywhere, and it didn't have to necessarily be a bad person —it could just be stumbling on a bear who was wandering around town, especially one with cubs or something. Or maybe accidentally waking up someone's dog.

"I just always thought it was a really nice thing to do. When you think about community service and helping others, usually you think about joining an organization and throwing some money at them or donating a few things out of your pantry or your closet. You don't really think about doing things yourself." She paused for a moment. "You know how much you have to look outside of yourself in order to see the needs that are around you to be a Secret Saint?"

Boy, did she ever. She hadn't paid such close attention to people in her entire life. She really did have to not only listen to conversations but keep her eyes open for things that people might need. And then try to figure out what exactly would make them happy. She didn't want to give things just for the sake of giving them. She wanted to give things that were necessary, and wanted, and would be used. Otherwise, it was just a waste of time and money, wasn't it?

"Yeah. You really have to focus on others."

"And that's why this type of thing is so good. Most of the time, we can kind of just skate along, doing the least amount possible, pretending to invest ourselves, when we're really not invested at all. We're just doing what we think is a good deed, we pat ourselves on the back, and then we go back to thinking about ourselves and our family and focusing on me, me, me all the time. It's not really truly investing in others the way being a Secret Saint is."

Now that Nelly had done it, she couldn't agree more.

"That is the kind of interest that keeps the community together. That is the kind of interest that Christians should show to especially other Christians but to the whole world. It's the kind of interest that Jesus has in us."

"And we're supposed to be like Jesus," she said.

"Exactly. We are supposed to be like Jesus."

They had moved into the kitchen by that time and almost had dinner prepped and ready to place on the table.

"You know, I hope you don't get so involved in your work that you don't keep an eye out for that special someone. God has someone for you." Her grandma seemed to be bringing that conversation up from out of nowhere.

Nelly was so shocked she couldn't say anything for a moment, and then she said, "If God brings me a lifetime partner, I will stop the Secret Saint and focus on him, because I do think that's what God wants us to do. To put our family first. After all, it's a lot more rewarding from a fleshly standpoint to help a whole pile of people who are appreciative than it is to just be there for your family." She knew it would feel more rewarding for her to go to her classroom than it would be for her to sit at home all day and watch her gram.

Although, if she didn't have to make money in order to continue with everything that she was doing, she might have considered it. She actually had considered taking a sabbatical year. But... She didn't know where her grandma would be in a year. Maybe her grandma would need her more next year than she would this coming year.

"Trust me, I am not going to close my heart or my mind to anyone that God puts in my path." But she did want to make sure that it was the right one. She had a couple of false alarms earlier in her twenties, and she didn't want to get emotionally involved with someone who wasn't living for the Lord and wanting to put Him first. She had almost made a bad decision at one point, and that was definitely something that she had learned from that failed relationship. God came first.

"Sometimes love grows in unexpected places," her gram said, smiling as she turned to get milk out of the refrigerator.

Well, the Secret Saint would certainly be an unexpected place. But she didn't know anything at all about the Secret Saint that she was working with, other than he was tall, had working man's hands, and seemed to be good at working with them.

Still, she tucked that idea away to think about. And she couldn't help the excitement that bubbled up. She might actually be meeting him again. She wouldn't mind having a helper. Or a coworker, more likely, since he wouldn't consider her his helper any more than she would consider him hers.

She couldn't wait until midnight tonight.

Chapter Ten

Roland walked slowly through town, staying in the shadows, keeping his eye on the gazebo in the park right in the middle of the town square.

There was no traffic, no one on the sidewalks, but he still avoided them to stay out of the light. He had been watching for the last thirty minutes, since 11:30, changing his vantage point every so often to make it less likely that someone could sneak up on him.

This was not exactly his forte. He wasn't that great at sneaking around. He was better at joking around, being a goofball, having fun with his nieces and nephews, and then sending them home to their parents while he ate junk food and relaxed.

Regardless, he did want to be careful. And he'd come to the conclusion that the other Secret Saint had invited him, so if they wanted him to show up, they were going to have to show up first. That was the burden when one was the person issuing the invitation. If they showed up, he would too.

It was five till twelve when he noticed movement in the shadow over by the fountain. It was not far from the gazebo, and he wished that he were somehow over on the other side, because he would be able to see better. Instead of moving, though, he froze, hoping his dark clothing allowed him to blend into the shadows while he watched one shadow detach itself from the others and move fluidly toward the gazebo. Long cape, deep hood, small stature.

It was the same woman he had worked with before. He was almost positive.

She stopped at the gazebo and then walked in, standing along the side so that anyone looking toward the town square would not notice an extra shadow on the inside of the gazebo.

If he hadn't known she was there, he wouldn't realize she was. She was good at hiding. He wondered if that was something she had practiced, or if it was just a natural thing.

Regardless, he didn't see any point in keeping her waiting, even though it was four minutes until midnight.

He moved out of the shadows, skirting around the edge of the square, until he was at the closest route so he would walk through the least amount of open area to the gazebo.

She saw him coming, because she moved, turning toward him, and her head moved with his movements.

"Good evening," he said as he reached the gazebo entrance.

"Good evening. I didn't realize the square was as well lit as it is."

"The gazebo is nice and dark though. We should be able to talk here without anyone seeing us. It's just coming and going."

"Yeah. If we...meet again, we'll have to pick a different spot."

He already had something in mind, but he just nodded for now.

"Thank you for coming. I wasn't sure you would."

"I wasn't sure I would either. But I'm intrigued. Partnership?"

"Yes," she said, and while he thought she had disguised her voice just a bit, it was obviously a woman's voice. He didn't try to pretend to be anything but a man, but he did try to disguise his voice, just slightly, in case this was someone he ran into in town. It would make things a lot less awkward if their identities stayed a secret.

"But I have a few conditions I would like to impose." She paused for a moment. "And I assume that you probably do too."

"That's correct. I definitely do not want anyone to find out my identity, including you. I just think that will keep things much less complicated."

"I agree. That was one of my conditions, so we're good there."

"That's great. I like it when we agree." He paused and figured they might as well continue with the conditions, although he had a bunch of questions swirling in his head. "What else?"

"That's probably the biggest one. I don't really have anything else. Other than...if we're going to communicate, we need to do it some way other than meeting here. And...we have to promise not to try to find out each other's identity. So, for example, if we're going to use an abandoned mailbox to exchange letters, you can't put a letter in and then sit and watch it for me to come get it."

"Agreed. I actually don't really want to know your identity, although I did wonder a little bit about you. Who exactly would I be working with? What kind of person?"

She laughed a bit. "I'm curious too, but I just wonder how many details we can exchange before we start to know each other too well, you know?"

"Exactly. I guess I'll tell you that I'm thirty. And I've lived in Mistletoe Meadows all my life. Doing the Secret Saint has enriched my life, caused me to think of others more than myself, and given me an awareness that I didn't have before. It also brings a joy to my life that I wasn't expecting. A sense of satisfaction and contentment that I didn't know was possible. Yes, I think God sees and rewards our works done in secret, but more than that, it makes me feel good, and I know I'm pleasing the Lord as well, which is a goal of my life."

"You couldn't have said that any better for me too. I'm exactly the same way. It's so much fun to see needs and to meet them, to sacrifice my time and money and sleep in order to make other people smile. I... I have to admit that sometimes I stick around after I've done something if I think there's an opportunity for me to see people's happiness. That gives me a high that drugs—well, I've never done drugs, so I don't really know what kind of a high they give you—but it feels like it's better than any kind of narcotics you could possibly take. And I want to praise the Lord. That's a goal of my life as well." She laughed for a moment, and then she said, "And you're not supposed to ask a woman's age or weight, but…I'm thirty."

So she was his age. He had been hoping she would say that, just so he would have an idea. He…didn't want to admit to himself that he might already have feelings for this person and he wanted to know that she wasn't a grandmother, at least, or a freshman in high school. He could tell from the way she talked that she wasn't that young, but he would have pegged her more at early twenties than thirty.

"Thank you for the information. I admit to being curious."

"Did I satisfy your curiosity?" she asked, like it was important to her for him to be content.

"You did. I hoped that we were both doing this for the Lord, not for ourselves, and I did kind of wonder what your age was. I suppose other than that, we don't really need to know anything else."

"No. I guess we don't."

"Other than where to meet, and how we're going to partner together."

"Of course. I was thinking personal things. The rest of this is just business."

"So let's get down to business," he said, wanting to talk to her more, but there was a warning in his brain that said that if he got too personal, it would be hard to keep his identity hidden, and that was something that was very important to him—to stay anonymous.

"Well, I've been thinking about this, and I'm certainly open to suggestions, but I have kind of a rough framework that I can present."

"Sounds good. I have a few ideas of my own, but you're the one who took the first step and suggested that we meet, so you lay out what you're thinking." He moved slightly, and she turned as well, sitting down on the bench so that she faced him.

After she was comfortable, he sat as well. There was no need for them to stand, although he did continue to look around. Although, there was nothing wrong with two people meeting in a gazebo and talking. There certainly were no laws against it, and there was no reason for anyone to think that they were the Secret Saints.

He hadn't made any deliveries tonight, although he didn't know about her. But it was less important that people not see them now that they were together. As far as he knew, people assumed there was one Secret Saint.

"All right. This is what I think. Just from working with you with the wood, I got the feeling that you're someone who works with your hands."

"That's accurate."

"And that you can do handy jobs, like fix-it jobs around the house? That older people might need, or that people might not be able to afford to hire a handyman for."

"That's true. I'm—" He closed his mouth immediately. He was almost going to say that he had been doing handyman jobs around his mother's house for years and that he had helped his family with various jobs as well, including roofing and putting additions onto homes, but he stopped just in time. He didn't want to give her information that would identify him. He had to keep his guard up, no matter how disarming she might be. Although, he did not believe that she was being disarming in order to try to get him to give her information.

"All right. My expertise is more in knowing children's Christmas lists, being able to buy groceries, and other things. And I'm very good at organizing and not so bad at decorating. I have a really vast supply network, and I can get a lot of donations without revealing my identity."

"I have quite an extensive network of supplies as well, but you're right about the organizing and decorating, and children are definitely not my forte. It sounds like we would work well together."

"Yes. I was thinking that. I know of several large projects that I would like to have done, but I haven't been able to because they're beyond my skill level, and hiring someone to do it is a little bit different than having a volunteer."

"All right. I suppose you know about the Kowalskis?"

"Yes. And the fact that their gutters are falling down and their shutters need to be rehung?"

"Exactly."

"I know."

"I would do it, but it's gonna require some pounding, and that's not exactly something you can sneak up and do in the middle of the night without waking people."

"Actually, they're going away all day tomorrow to visit their son and daughter who live in Maryland for a Christmas celebration with them. Their son couldn't get off over Christmas, so they're heading up there early. But just overnight. They'll be back the next day."

"All right. Perfect." Wow, her sources were really good. "So we have a one-night opening."

"Yes. And I can have all the supplies that you need."

"I'll have to check, but I think I can get everything."

"I can come and give you a hand—I don't know how much help I'll be with the actual work."

"Just knowing when an available time is is actually a huge help, because I didn't know that they were leaving."

He couldn't see inside her hood enough to know whether she smiled or not, but there seemed to be a loosening in her body language, and he thought she was pleased, like she was pulling her own weight.

He was impressed with her knowledge and truly with her organization as well.

"There are a few other jobs that are small like that that need to be done, and I've been keeping an ear to the ground to try to figure out when people will be leaving so they could be slipped in. There's also a porch that needs to be replaced, but that's not exactly the kind of job one can do without permission. I've been trying to figure out—"

"Are you talking about the Martins?"

"Yes," she said, nodding eagerly.

"I know them, and I have a couple contacts. We can probably get permission. But I still think it would be nice to try to do it when they're not around. Although... I'm not sure that's something we can do in a night."

"No. Probably not, although you would know that better than me."

"And that will require a lot of material. A little bit more planning. We'll have to keep that one in our pocket and think about it for a bit."

She nodded, going along with what he suggested.

They talked a bit more about a few other families that they both knew, but the Kowalskis were the first on the list. He didn't know about her, but the more he talked to her, the more he was impressed with her, the thought that she had been putting into this, as well as her extensive network of information. It rivaled his and maybe even surpassed it.

Finally, when they'd been talking for almost two hours, Roland reluctantly stood.

She stood with him and then gasped. "One of the things we forgot to talk about—how we were going to communicate. We can't give each other our cell phone numbers."

"No. Absolutely not." They might find out that they already had each other's numbers or something equally horrifying.

"But I don't know what to do. I did give it some thought, and I was thinking the gazebo would work, but it's in the middle of town. Not the best place at all."

"No. I'll tell you what, follow me." He'd been thinking about this for a while, and he really thought his idea would probably work, although not nearly as good as messaging or texting, of course. That would be best if keeping their identities a secret wasn't so important.

She hesitated a bit, and he realized that she was a woman alone with a man she didn't know. Would she trust him enough to follow him?

He wouldn't blame her if she didn't. He wasn't sure if he were her that he would. After all, she was much smaller than he was, and he could easily overpower her if he wanted to.

But the hesitation was just for a brief moment, and then she followed him out into the town square and onto the sidewalk. He slipped into the shadows, and she slipped there with him, her cloak rippling behind her as a soft breeze picked it up as they walked through a few areas where the snow had not melted.

It was cold enough for the ground to freeze back up, so he wasn't concerned about making footprints anywhere. But he did watch for icy spots.

Finally, they were on the outside of town, on the opposite end from which he had parked, near an old tree that had been struck by lightning a few years prior.

"There's a hole here in this tree. I...happened to notice it this summer when the kids were playing ball and one of them kicked it way too hard. I ended up running over here and seeing this hole. It's...not big enough for an animal to have a nest in, but it would be big enough for a note." He put his finger in the hole and wiggled it.

"That's perfect. I think we could get an entire piece of paper in there, and if we're careful, we could completely hide it so that no one else would accidentally find it."

"Exactly. I found the note that you left on the porch, but anyone else could have found it too."

"I know. I wish I could have waited longer, but I just couldn't."

He let that go. He didn't know why she couldn't wait longer or anything about her, but...he really admired and respected her just from the conversation they'd had this evening.

"All right then. I'll try to make a point of coming to check on this once a day if I can."

"Me too. I usually take a walk in the morning, and I can make sure that my route ensures that I swing by this tree. It might be a little bit more touch and go in the evening though.”

“All right. When I come, it will probably be after I’m done with a Secret Saint delivery or around noon. So it looks like we won’t meet each other.”

“That’s important,” she agreed.

“We could also try to make sure that we are dressed in our disguises.” He indicated his ski mask and her cloak. “If we haven’t made specific plans to meet, we can meet here at midnight and discuss what we’re going to do.”

“All right. That sounds good. I don’t do something every night. I just couldn’t.”

“Me either. If we do the Kowalskis tomorrow night, I probably won’t do anything the next night, but I could meet you and discuss what we found and organize something else.”

“That sounds perfect. Every other night or every two nights. Maybe as we get closer to Christmas a little bit more often, but... work one night, meet one night.”

“Yes. Meet here, leave a note if anything has changed since the last time we talked that can’t wait until we talk again.”

She nodded. “That sounds perfect. I... I’m kind of excited about it. I know this is maybe immature on my part, but it’s made everything more interesting. A secret meeting tree, a little hole to put our notes, meeting times, it’s...super fun.”

“Yeah. I’ve always looked forward to doing this, and I’ve really been enjoying it, but this has definitely knocked it up a few levels. I... I’m more excited about it now than I had been when I first started.”

She couldn’t see his mouth, but he was grinning at her, and he assumed that she was probably smiling back. He wanted to picture her sparkling eyes, but he had a little bit of trouble. Were they blue? Green? Maybe a deep shade of walnut brown? He wasn’t sure, and for some reason, he was more tempted than he had been all evening to pull her cloak back and look deep into them.

But he resisted the urge. After all, that would be a huge betrayal of trust. It didn't matter how much he wanted to, he certainly wasn't going to.

"All right, tomorrow, at the Kowalskis' house at midnight. If anything changes before that, I'll leave a note or you will, and I won't start on anything until we see each other at the Kowalskis', just to confirm that everything's a go."

"Yes. That sounds good."

"All right then. See you tomorrow night."

She nodded, and then she turned, her cloak swirling as she strode away in the exact opposite direction that he had parked his truck.

They'd even coordinated that without realizing it, parking in complete opposite directions.

Something told him that they were going to be really, really good together.

Chapter Eleven

Nelly couldn't believe that she had actually done it. She'd talked to the other Secret Saint, and they had decided to work together! She was pretty much walking on air the entire next day. Some of her kids noticed and commented that she seemed happier than usual.

She even let the kids stay out an extra ten minutes at recess.

She had walked around the tree on her morning walk, although she hadn't stopped to check it on the way past to begin with. Rather, she kept a lookout for anyone who looked like they might be about the same height and build as the man she had talked to last night. She believed him and trusted him, but...trust and verify? Something like that.

Regardless, she hadn't seen anything, so on her way back, she'd gone to the tree and looked in. There was nothing there, and she couldn't stop the little stab of disappointment. Not that she wanted there to be. She didn't want any changes at all to the plans that they'd already made. And she didn't have anything to leave, so she hardly expected anything from him. She walked away from the tree and continued on her walk.

She'd swing by again in the afternoon, and maybe she'd even check as she walked by the first time.

She thought the notes in the tree and meeting at midnight were really great ideas and was looking forward to working with him again.

Thankfully, her grandmother had another good evening, and they had some wonderful conversation as they worked together to make supper.

She had read online—and she had talked to the doctor in town, Dr. Terry, who had agreed—that when an older person was fighting off a cold or virus, sometimes they got a little confused.

She didn't remember her gram having any kind of symptoms of a cold or anything, but maybe she had been on the verge of getting one.

Whatever it was, she had been lucid for a really long time—for a lot of days in a row—and Nelly couldn't stop her feeling of anticipation that perhaps her gram wasn't going to be suffering from dementia after all.

She knew she was probably wishing on rainbows and unicorns, but she couldn't help grasping at every positive straw she possibly could.

She took a small nap in the evening after supper but was up by 11:30, dressed and ready to slip out of the house.

She hadn't told her gram that she was going anywhere and hoped that her gram would sleep soundly all night.

She felt like it was better for her to do as little talking about the Secret Saint as possible, even though her grandma seemed like she was doing well. Now that there was someone else involved, she had extra incentive to try to keep everything under wraps.

After considering that, she stayed with her decision to not tell her grandma about her partner in that endeavor. At least, if her gram accidentally told someone about her, she wouldn't be destroying his cover as well.

As she made her way to the Kowalski house, she tried to pick his figure out in the shadows. But she could not. However, she saw a truck parked in the alley behind the house, and she assumed that the supplies on the back were the ones that he was going to use to replace the shutters and possibly some of the gutters.

"Hey there," a voice said, low and soft.

She had walked right past him and hadn't seen him. "I'm sorry. I was looking at your truck. Looks like you have supplies."

"I sure do. I hoped maybe you would give me a hand carrying them to the house as I need them. Normally, I would have parked right where I was working and wouldn't worry too much about banging things around, but since we need to be quiet..."

"Of course. I'll help." She was a little worried that he was going to be doing all the work and she would just be standing around twiddling her thumbs. There wasn't much fun in that.

Except, he wouldn't know that tonight the Kowalskis weren't going to be home if it hadn't been for her, so she was contributing something.

They went to the truck together, and he told her what he was going to need first. He grabbed one end, she grabbed the other, and they carefully carried it around the house without making any noise at all.

The neighbors' houses weren't particularly close, but they were close enough that if they started making too much noise, they had a good chance of waking someone up.

"I actually put a cloth over my hammer, because while this shouldn't take too much hammering, it'll take enough, and that should muffle the sound," her partner said as they set the first piece down.

"That was really smart," she said, knowing that she wouldn't have thought of that, but she wasn't exactly a handyman either.

They worked in silence for a little bit with their natural division of labor and efficient coordination seeming to come without them thinking about it at all.

"I never thought I would be doing this at any point in my life," she said at one point.

He was working on straightening up one of the shutters, and she was standing guard, to make sure that she didn't see anyone coming.

He grunted. "Me either. My siblings would never believe that I'm here right now doing this."

He had siblings. She tucked that information away without meaning to.

"That's not your reputation?"

"Not in my family. Older siblings have a tendency to look down on the younger ones and think they're immature, no matter how old you get, you know?"

"I guess I don't really know. I'm an only child." Her grandma had raised her for most of her life. Her mom had been in and out, rather unsteady, and her dad had been nonexistent.

"Oh, I'm sorry. That's too bad."

"Actually, I enjoyed it." She looked at his shoulder. "I guess you don't know what you're missing when you don't have siblings. And actually, the idea is a little...not fun. After all, you'd have to share everything for one thing."

"Yeah, but you always have a playmate for anything."

"Did your siblings always want to play when you did?" she asked, knowing that it was true in the classroom—even best friends didn't get along all the time.

"No. Good point." He sighed. "I just can't imagine not having my siblings. But you're right, you wouldn't have to share, and sometimes you didn't have playmates, even if you did have siblings, and they did take some of your parents' attention away."

"Yeah. There's that. I got full attention from my grandma, and I really benefited from that, I think. I was always a little bit more mature than other kids my age, I think." Except for her competition with Roland, but she didn't want thoughts of Roland to ruin her time with her Secret Saint partner, so she shoved that aside. Everyone was entitled to a little bit of immaturity, right?

"I was probably less mature than other kids my age. Although, I don't know. There definitely were lessons that I learned in a big family that other kids didn't learn, so it probably balanced itself out."

If those were lessons in how to be a handyman, he certainly had learned them well. He had the shutters fixed and straightened and reattached, and the gutters all fixed, along with replacing one section that had rotted out at the bottom.

"I've been wanting to do that for a while. I'm so glad that you knew that they wouldn't be home today. It irritated me every time I saw it. Not because it was an eyesore, but because I knew I could fix it, I just didn't want to do it as myself, you know?"

"Being a Secret Saint kind of spoils you. You…enjoy doing kind things and just clutching the knowledge close to your chest without sharing it with anyone. At least I do."

"I agree with you completely. I wouldn't want to do anything with my name attached to it, although…somehow you get suckered into doing different things for the community anyway."

She laughed, thinking about how she got suckered into volunteering to head the church play. That wasn't so bad, but doing it with Roland… She didn't even want to think about it.

"I know what you mean. Although, I suppose it's probably good to do things where people can watch you too, because kids need role models, you know?"

"That's true. Your nieces and nephews and children if you have any."

She laughed. "I'm not married. And I don't have any children." Unless one counted the kids she had in the classroom, which she almost said, and then she clamped her mouth closed. She didn't want him to figure out who she was, and if she said she had kids in the classroom, that would narrow it down to the teachers at the school. It would be pretty easy to figure out at that point, because there weren't that many teachers who weren't married and didn't have any children.

That was a close one. Although, the more time she spent with him, the less concerned she was about him knowing her identity. She...trusted him.

"All right, I think that's pretty much it," her partner said just a half an hour later.

She was a little disappointed that their time had come to an end, although she was getting tired again.

"I have a few ideas of what our next project could be." He rattled off a few people who they could help. "Let's think about it and meet tomorrow night at midnight to talk about it. Okay?"

She nodded, agreeing with him about several that he mentioned and then being surprised at another one. She'd have to check that one out. "That sounds good to me. I'll see you tomorrow night at midnight."

He nodded. "And if I hear anything about the Kowalskis' reaction, I'll be sure to let you know then."

Wow. She wasn't expecting that. "Thanks. It's always so much fun to hear that it was really a blessing. If I hear anything, I'll be sure to let you know too." Since tomorrow, or actually today, was Saturday, she wouldn't have as many contacts as she usually did at school, but she would still be taking her walk and possibly talking to people. She'd definitely keep an ear out, because it wasn't just her that was benefiting anymore. It was actually even more fun to work with someone and share the fun and contentment and satisfaction of making people smile with them.

To her surprise, she was sad as they walked away from each other.

Chapter Twelve

*S*aturday afternoon, they had another Christmas planning meeting. Honestly, Roland was trying to figure out how to get out of going. The last time, he had such a hard time not telling Nelly how silly she was being that he wasn't sure whether he would be able to hold his temper and his words in this time.

She wanted to spend money on all the things that were not important and had no clue that they would bring in new people if they did new things.

Of course he wanted to do something that was associated with Christmas, and of course he wanted to tell the Christmas story, but they didn't have to do the same exact thing year after year after year.

He tried to calm himself down as he stepped inside the church. It was not going to go over well if he was worked up before he even saw her.

He thought about how well he worked with the Secret Saint and how difficult it was to work with Nelly. Too bad the Secret Saint couldn't be in charge of the Christmas program. They worked so well together that the Christmas program would be perfect for them.

As he walked in, he noticed the program fund collection container sitting right inside the door in the vestibule.

Everyone knew the church doors weren't locked, and...that didn't seem like a very smart place to put it, if anyone came during the day and dropped a rather large donation in.

On that thought, he walked over just to check to see if there was anything in it.

He was leaning over it looking when the door opened and Mrs. Tucker walked in.

"What are you doing?" Mrs. Tucker said, looking at him like he had a spider on his nose.

It didn't help that he whipped around like he was guilty of doing something bad. She just spoke to him in such a shrill voice that it scared him.

"Just checking out the collection container. It doesn't seem like a very good place to put it. The doors are never locked, and anyone could walk away with it."

"You're absolutely right. In fact, I thought that was what you might be doing," she said. "Were you getting ready to take it?"

Mrs. Tucker had taught him first through third grade every Sunday morning in Sunday school. He had to admit, he was not the best-behaved child ever, and more than once, his parents had had to discipline him when he had gotten home because Mrs. Tucker told his mother that he was not being good.

It was just so fun to be bad in her class, and he wasn't even sure why.

But Mrs. Tucker had not been endeared to him ever after.

Of course, Nelly had been in the class too, and that was ninety percent of the reason why he had such a hard time being good. That was before their Valentine's Day debacle, or at least mostly, and... now that he thought about it, he kind of had a little crush on her.

Maybe the whole Valentine's Day thing came about because he was jealous that she had given such a nice valentine to Tommy Peterson.

"Why don't we go in now," Mrs. Tucker said, waiting for him to step into the sanctuary first.

It irritated him that she was treating him like he was in first grade again, like he hadn't had a spotless reputation ever since he'd been in her Sunday school class. Well, except for a few youthful indiscretions, which happened to every child, and also the whole competition with Nelly, and the fact that he had older siblings who treated him like a baby.

But beyond all that, there was absolutely no chance that anyone would suspect that he would swipe money out of the collection. It was annoying that she acted like he would.

"Oh, look who shows up. Late," he heard Nelly mutter under her breath as he walked in. To his consternation, he noticed that everyone else was there.

"Mrs. Tucker came in after me," he volunteered in a low tone as he walked by her.

The pastor cleared his throat, and Mrs. Tucker said, "I was late because I was volunteering at Helping Hands Daycare, thank you very much. And I had told Pastor Connelly that I was going to be late. What's your excuse?"

Well, that didn't go over very well. Normally, he was a little bit more charming than what he had been with Mrs. Tucker, and he hadn't realized that he was late. He'd had one family at the Christmas tree farm, and he couldn't leave until they bought a tree. They went around and looked at every single tree before they came back and cut down the first one they'd seen.

It just took forever, and he wasn't able to leave. His mom was watching the place, but he didn't want to leave whenever he knew that a family might need help.

His mom still didn't look very good to him, although no one in his family seemed to care other than him, so he'd quit saying anything.

Still, he wasn't going to try to defend himself. Not to Mrs. Tucker. Because he certainly didn't have an excuse like she did.

"I'd like to call this meeting to order," Pastor Connelly said as he stood up, and Roland slid into the closest seat, which happened to be right beside Nelly.

Normally, he would have chosen the seat furthest away from her, but the pastor only had six chairs set up, and there was one empty chair clear over on the other side, but for him to walk the whole way down the row of five chairs and plop into that one would be rather obvious that he was trying to avoid her. And considering that they were supposed to be doing this together, he felt like that was probably not the wise course of action for him to take.

When no one said anything right away, Roland figured he could start. "Pastor, I feel like we need to spend some money on new costumes. Costumes make or break the program, and the ones that we have are just so old. We don't even have to spend a whole lot of money on them—we could sew them ourselves."

"We don't have enough time to sew them before the program," Mrs. Tucker interrupted.

"And why would we spend money on new costumes when what we really need are new people? That means spending money on marketing. That's where the money should go. We should definitely allocate way more for marketing and advertising avenues that we haven't done before." That was just common sense. Although now he wished he would have sat down at the end of the row, as Nelly shot him a look of pure venom.

"No one who listens to the radio is going to come to a church program just because we put a commercial on. But the people who are here watching it would like to be entertained with something that is beautiful and lovely, and we can't do beautiful and lovely with costumes that are thirty years old!" She might have been a little heated, but that matched his current state of mind.

"It doesn't matter how old the costumes are. If we're doing the same tired old thing with Mary and Joseph, then those costumes will work just fine—in fact, tired old costumes for the same tired old thing."

"You think the Christmas story is tired and old? Maybe you're not the right person for this job," Nelly said.

He didn't mean it the way she took it.

"I didn't mean that the Christmas story was tired and old. I meant that doing the same thing every year, year after year, is tired and old."

"That's what Christmas is! The same thing every year!" Nelly lifted a hand in frustration and then looked at Pastor Connelly, pleading with him to help her. "I'm not sure I can do this."

It was quiet after she stopped speaking. Obviously the other committee members were very uncomfortable with their outburst. Roland felt a little bit bad, especially because he really didn't want to make everyone else feel awkward or uncomfortable, but at the same time, he was absolutely right.

Nelly was probably just arguing with him for the sake of arguing, and now she was trying to make him look bad, which he definitely didn't need in front of Mrs. Tucker who already thought he was stealing money out of the collection box.

"It's fine. We can buy new outfits, I don't care. It's just not a wise use of the money. That's all. But we can waste it if you want to."

That was definitely not the best wording that he'd ever used in his life, and in fact, he thought he probably should have been a little more careful with his words, because if Nelly looked annoyed before, there was practically steam coming out of her ears now.

"I'm not even sure we're going to have any money to buy anything. Donations have been down this year," Pastor Connelly interrupted their conversation, and all eyes went to him.

"Oh. I'm sorry. I didn't know," Nelly said after a moment of silence from everyone else.

"Yeah, me either," he said, thinking to himself that it was quite possible that someone had stolen money out of the box, the way it was sitting there, but he didn't want to say that, since Mrs. Tucker had seen him looking at it, and he didn't want her to be thinking any more about someone stealing money. Plus, he had absolutely no evidence that anyone might have been doing that. It was just conjecture on his part, and in his experience, throwing out accusations that weren't based in fact that one hadn't checked to be sure about was wildly inappropriate and reckless.

"Does anyone have any suggestions on fundraising that we could do with immediate benefits? We should not have left this until the last minute, and again, I have to take the blame for it, since my wife was ill, and I didn't get on this the way I should have."

"Well, Nelly always spearheads it. She could have said something." Mrs. Brown spoke for the first time.

Roland grunted in approval, which earned him a withering glance from Nelly.

He was totally immune to her looks, and he looked at her coolly and then looked back at Pastor Connelly, letting her know how unaffected he was by her withering stares.

In reality, she did look kind of fearsome, and he felt a little bit bad for her. She had plenty of things on her plate with teaching school and all the things she was doing there. His nephew couldn't say enough good things about her, and his family gushed over her as well. So as annoyed as he was with her, and as much as he wished that he was working with someone who was easy to work with, like the Secret Saint, he supposed he ought to try to adjust his attitude. Especially when Mrs. Brown started knocking her.

"I'm really not sure. Usually, we put a box out, and we get more money than we could possibly use. In fact, we often end up sending the extra money to overseas missions. I don't know why it would be different this year," Nelly said, sounding truly confused.

Roland didn't feel like he had won the argument, and even though he knew it was not wise to open his mouth again, he couldn't help but say, "But if we do have anything extra, my vote definitely goes toward using it for marketing."

Nelly rolled her eyes, crossed her arms over her chest, and began a conversation with Mrs. Brown and Mrs. Tucker about what they could do to earn money.

"I think we could probably just keep the box where it is and make sure that you announce it from the pulpit on Sunday. If we haven't had trouble getting donations before, maybe people were just a little blindsided because we are doing it in a shorter period of time, and it's closer to Christmas."

He could see Mrs. Tucker narrowing her eyes and looking suspiciously at him.

He wanted to roll his eyes, but he didn't. That wouldn't have been very kind.

They spoke for another thirty minutes before the meeting finally broke up. He knew he should stay and politely make small talk and then hold the door for the ladies as they left, but he wanted to go home and relieve his mother of her duties. This time of year, their busiest hours were in the evening just before dark as people got home from work, ate supper, and then bundled the kids up to go get a tree.

He didn't want his mother to have to be out in the cold any longer than what she already had been.

And he couldn't deny that he was eager to meet with his Secret Saint partner at midnight too. That thought bolstered him as he left, feeling rather sour in his stomach at the way the meeting had gone but even more so at the way he had acted. He hadn't represented Jesus very well at all. In fact, if anything, he had been downright mean, insisting on his own way, when a compromise, or at least a kind word before he suggested his own idea, could have been much nicer.

He knew he was just clay and couldn't expect perfection, but he said a small prayer that God would help him to do better. Because he really needed to learn to love Nelly as a sister in Christ and stop being so irritated every time she opened her mouth.

At least he could look forward to meeting with someone that he didn't have any problems getting along with later this evening. And that made him smile.

Chapter Thirteen

elly walked wearily to the tree where she was to meet her Secret Saint partner.

The church committee meeting had gone horribly. She'd never had a church meeting go that badly, and it was all Roland McBride's fault.

How he even managed to get on the committee in the first place was a mystery. Anyone who could be so rude and nasty didn't deserve to be on a committee. He needed to be sitting in the pew hearing the sermon and applying it to his life!

She tried to stop herself from thinking that way, because she hadn't exactly shown her best side, and she definitely hadn't represented Jesus very well at all. In fact, if she were being completely honest, she owed the man an apology.

Why couldn't he be as easy to work with as the Secret Saint was? They just jived in a way she never had with anyone before. And honestly, she'd been looking forward since yesterday to meeting him again.

Unlike Roland, who had been late for the meeting, the Secret Saint was early, standing beside the tree, waiting on her.

"It's so nice to be with a coworker who arrives early. Thank you," she said by way of greeting.

"Rough day?" he asked. His voice sounded calm and soothing, and she took comfort in it.

"Oh goodness," she said, trying to remember that she couldn't give away too many details. "I have...a coworker...who is just so frustrating."

She didn't know whether Roland was technically a coworker, but she did have to work with him, and they were supposed to be doing the committee stuff together. So she felt like the term wasn't a lie.

"That's too bad. I know what you mean. I'm reeling from a clash with my own coworker. So unreasonable and frustrating."

"I'm sorry. That sounds terrible."

"It sounds like you know exactly what I'm talking about. What's the problem?"

"Oh goodness, he's just so frustrating. You know how you don't mesh with someone? How you just don't get along, and you rub each other the wrong way pretty much every time you see each other?"

"Yeah. I totally know exactly what you mean."

"Yeah. That's just the kind of person that I have to work with, and unfortunately, over Christmas, you often get thrown together with people that you don't usually get thrown together with, and that's just one of the things you have to deal with. I wish this person would get some Christmas spirit and start to be at least a little kind."

"Same. Although, I have to admit after I got home today, I looked back on my behavior, and I realized that I could use some improvement."

Immediately that made her feel bad. She'd been complaining and had totally left out her part. "That's funny. Because I did the same thing. You know how God sometimes puts people in your path, and He's like, 'Okay, let's see you get along with this person,' and you're like, 'Really, Lord? Could You give me someone nice?' And you realize that He's done this because He wants you to not just show the love of

Jesus to everyone but become more like Jesus by loving people who feel unlovable."

"That's a really great point. I was focusing more on myself and how I needed to reflect Jesus in everything that I did, but...I wasn't successful today, that's for sure. But you're right, I think He puts people like that in our lives on purpose."

She hadn't really considered it before, but God had had Roland McBride in her life almost her entire life, and he really had inspired her to be better, despite the fact that he was the most unlikable person she knew.

"I'm sorry. I didn't mean to dump on you," she finally said after they'd been quiet for a bit.

"No, it's okay. I guess you've inspired me to try to look for places where God might be trying to cause me to be a better person. I want to point my finger at the other person and say they're the ones who need to grow up, but I could do better too."

She appreciated his compliment and felt like she could return it. "I feel like you make me better in a good way. Without making me feel frustrated and angry, you just point out areas or things that I can do that would make me more like Jesus."

"Well, I might have some difficult relationships in the rest of my life, but this is what I look forward to. I'm glad we decided to work together."

"Me too. And speaking of which, I heard about the Hatter family and that their son's been in the hospital."

"I was just going to tell you about that," he said.

She laughed. She loved how they thought the same way and seemed to have similar ideas and thoughts. So much more compatible than Roland.

She needed to push him aside, though, because she didn't want him to ruin her entire day. She wanted to enjoy this time with her partner.

"I felt like they could use some gas cards, and I put out some feelers for donations. After all, the hospital is an hour and a half away, and they're making the trip five times a week."

"Yeah. That's a great idea. I hadn't thought about that. I've been thinking more about decorating the outside of their house, which hasn't been done, and I've heard from several sources that it's really bothered Mrs. Hatter that she hadn't been able to put up decorations. It would also make the kids happy."

"I don't suppose they have a Christmas tree yet? I hadn't thought to ask."

"No. They don't."

"I can bring one with me. That is not a problem," he said. She could hear a grin in his voice.

"Perfect."

They continued to talk about a few other things that they could do, with her partner thinking about the practical needs and Nelly moving more along with items that were decorative and comforting.

The seamless way they worked together eased the stress that she felt over her daytime interaction with Roland.

"Well, that sounds good. I think we could have all of that ready by tomorrow. They should be getting back in the afternoon, and I bet they'll be tired. I'm guessing they'll be in bed early."

"Still start at midnight?" he asked.

"Yes, if that works for you?"

"It does." Her partner paused for just a moment and then said, "I just wanted to thank you. Working with you feels so easy, and especially after the horrendous time I had today with other people I have to work with, it's just been really nice to get to be with someone that I'm so compatible with."

"Same." She could feel the tension of the day draining out of her after being with him for a little while. "It just feels so good and enjoyable to be with you. I didn't realize when we agreed to work together that it was going to be like this. I look forward to it, to be honest."

"I do too. It's been a blessing."

"I'm looking forward to seeing you tomorrow night."

"Same."

She smiled and then raised a hand, waving before she turned around and walked back toward her vehicle. She had parked in the same place she had before, because she noticed that he parked at exactly the opposite spot. It was funny that they coordinated so well, because they did it again. She started walking one direction, and after a moment, she could hear his footsteps receding in the other.

It felt good and right to be working with someone like him, and she smiled to herself. What a lovely meeting. So much different than the committee meeting at church.

Which was a little bit sad, since it was a church meeting. It should have gone better. And it was partly her fault. She needed to do better.

Chapter Fourteen

"So how's the whole Secret Saint thing going?" Judd asked as Roland watched the last customer walk to their car with their Christmas tree and a wreath that they bought on the spur of the moment.

Normally his mother made a lot more wreaths to sell, but she hadn't made nearly as many as she usually did. He tried not to think about what that could mean but instead focused on the fact that he was going to try to slip away in ten minutes to go pick up Robert and his two siblings, since Summer had a client coming and she would be doing her horse therapy that afternoon.

It wasn't that the kids couldn't stay there—they could—but often they would go hang out at Grandma's house, only Roland had offered to take the kids to the Christmas tree farm and let them help out with him, and Marjorie hadn't argued with him at all. Which was very unusual and fueled the worry that had been nagging in his brain for the last few weeks.

He shook that aside though and focused on Judd.

"I actually got a partner." Judd was the one person in the world he could talk to about that. Although of course he wasn't going to spill his partner's identity—if he could, although it would be hard to do since he had no idea who she was.

"Really?" Judd seemed surprised.

"Yeah. We work together really well. She has a lot of strengths where I have weaknesses, and I'm able to do a lot of handyman things that she had been skipping over. Her contacts are amazing. Plus, she's a lot more organized than I am."

"Wow. It's not Nelly Bushnell, is it?"

Roland stared at Judd, his eyes going wide, before he started to laugh. "Oh my goodness, no way! If you had been at any of the church committee meetings or yesterday's play practice, you wouldn't even think about suggesting that. My word, that woman could cause a saint to lose his sainthood. Holy smokes. Ha ha."

"And you don't think it has anything to do with the fact that the two of you don't get along," Judd said easily with the casual confidence of someone who knew him well enough that he could say things that perhaps might offend someone who they didn't know as well.

"Okay, you're right. She just rubs me the wrong way. Actually, the exact opposite of my Secret Saint partner, who is a female, by the way. But...it's just night and day difference. I get along with this person, we work so well together. She makes me feel calm and secure and brings out the best in me. Nelly, on the other hand, makes me feel stressed and angry and brings out the worst in me."

Judd laughed. "Sometimes it's all in our own attitude."

That gave him pause, and he had to admit Judd had a point. Attitude had a huge role in how he thought and felt. "You're right. I know that my attitude toward Nelly is not the right way that I should act, and I've been praying that I can be more like Jesus when I'm around her. It's...a long, hard road though." He rolled his eyes.

"Yeah. I don't know what to tell you other than just keep working at it. God puts people in our lives for a reason, and sometimes that reason is so that we can work on areas of our personality that need a little attention."

"Interesting. I've heard that before. And I agree."

They chatted a bit more, with Roland being tempted to mention his mother, but he didn't, because the last few times he mentioned it, everyone acted like he was nuts.

Shortly thereafter, he drove down the roadways to pick up his niece and nephews.

He followed a car in and realized as they parked beside each other that it was Nelly.

Seriously? He had to meet her here of all places?

And then he realized there was a kid he didn't recognize in the back of her car. She must be the one bringing the kid for therapy.

He got out of the car and walked toward the barn, since he'd seen all three kids waiting for him there, along with Summer and Gilbert as well.

He didn't wait for Nelly to get out of her car, wanting to chat with his sister-in-law and his brother before she got there and then cut out, possibly without having to talk to her.

"You seem like you're in a rush," Summer said as she looked up from the horse she was leading in from the pasture.

"No. Not really. You guys ready?" he said to the kids.

They cheered and said yes, and then ran for his car.

"Looks like your client is here, so I don't want to hold you up."

"Yeah, I'm so glad that Nelly has taken an interest in her. She's actually even paying for the lessons, if you can believe it," Summer said in a lower tone as Nelly walked their way.

Really? Nelly was actually paying for the therapy?

"It's one of her students. She's noticed that she struggles in class, and then she found out that there are some things going on at home. I can't talk about that, but...Nelly is definitely a really amazing person," Summer said. Being that she hadn't grown up here and wasn't the same age as Roland, she probably didn't know about all of the competition that had gone on between Nelly and him growing up. Maybe she'd heard snippets of it in family conversations, but she'd probably forgotten. Otherwise, she probably wouldn't be saying such wonderful things about Nelly in front of him.

Or maybe she would, trying to convince him that Nelly was a good person.

"Hey there, I've got Allie with me," Nelly said as she walked up to Summer.

She gave Roland a side glance and lifted her head, which probably was a greeting but looked more to him like she was sticking her nose in the air.

Play practice the night before hadn't gone the best.

"Good to see you guys. I'll be skipping out. I'll pick the kids up when I'm done with my meeting," Gilbert said as he waved a hand at Roland.

"I'll be leaving you guys too. See ya," he said, trying to be nice to Nelly but able to see from Summer's glance that he hadn't quite succeeded.

She had narrowed her eyes, but there was also a bit of interest in her gaze as she looked between Roland and Nelly.

He could tell her immediately that there was nothing going on in that department, because he could tell a matchmaking gaze when he saw it, and he didn't appreciate having one directed between Nelly and him. It was all he could do to be nice to her—he certainly wasn't interested in spending any extra time with her and absolutely not interested in any kind of romantic relationship.

Somehow, when he thought about a romantic relationship, the idea of his Secret Saint partner flashed across his mind.

He really didn't even know who she was. How could he be developing feelings for her?

But he was—he was sure of it. He looked forward to seeing her, was sad when they were apart, and thought about her all the time when she wasn't around. He admired her dedication to the Lord and her desire to be a blessing to other people in the community. All the signs were there.

As he drove home with the kids, listening to their chatter and answering their questions, it was all he could do to not smile at the thought of meeting her in a few hours. He couldn't wait.

Chapter Fifteen

Nelly opened the door and set her bag down in its usual spot, feeling light and free. December was a fabulous month, and she had been having so much fun with her students in the classroom. Of course, they were still learning, but they were also making decorations and talking about what their families were going to do over the Christmas vacation, which was still weeks away but still exciting to think about. The anticipation, to Nelly, was some of the best parts of Christmas.

Of course, it probably didn't hurt that tonight she was going to be meeting with her Secret Saint partner. Of course not.

"Good evening, Gram. What a wonderful day!" she said as her gram shuffled over to the door.

"Who are you?" Gram said, and Nelly's spirits plummeted immediately.

Her gram didn't recognize her?

She'd been doing so well for so long that Nelly had almost convinced herself that whatever had been wrong with her gram had been just a temporary thing that her grandma had gotten through.

"Gram, it's me, Nelly."

"Is your horse parked outside?"

"What?" Nelly said, blinking. That threw her for a loop.

"You're not going to keep me in here. I can get out if I want to." She shuffled forward faster like she was going to plow through Nelly. Nelly wasn't sure what to do, and the door was still open. She reached forward, but before she could touch her gram, her grandma's foot must have caught on the coffee table at the end of the couch, and she lost her balance, tripping and crashing into the lamp, which flew to the floor, and she somehow managed to tip over the coffee table, although her gram leaned against the couch, not quite landing on the floor as Nelly rushed forward to grab a hold of her and help her.

"Let go of me! I'll scream for help!" Gram said.

Nelly had no idea what to do. Did she continue to try to help her gram to keep her from falling and breaking something? Or did she let her go so she wouldn't upset her?

What would that matter? Nelly wasn't doing anything wrong.

But her grandma was very agitated when she got near, so she tried to stay close, just in case her grandma lost her balance. She balanced on the arm of the couch, and for now, she was fine.

"Are you okay, Grandma?" she asked, really worried. Not just for Gram's mental issue, but had she hurt herself in all the confusion? She didn't think that she'd seen anything that would actually hurt her gram, but sometimes accidents could be really weird, and things happened so fast that it was easy to miss something.

"I'm just fine. Who are you again?"

"Is everything okay in here?" a voice asked from the open doorway.

It was a familiar voice, and as Nelly spun around, she understood why it was familiar.

Roland. Of course, he would be in the area. Looking past him, she could see a Christmas tree wrapped and lying on the porch. He must have been delivering it to someone.

Of all the people who could be going by when something was happening at her house, it would have to be him.

"Young man, this woman just walked into my house unannounced, and she was trying to grab me."

"Are you okay?" Roland asked, his voice calm and reassuring. His eyes flicked to Nelly, and he lifted his brows a little. He knew this was where she lived too. But he shook his head a bit and moved forward slowly. "Can I help you stand up, ma'am?"

"Yes, please. It's so nice that there are still kind people in the world." She sighed. "Sometimes I just don't know how clumsy I can be."

Roland walked around Nelly and took a hold of her gram's elbow, carefully straightening her from the arm of the couch while Nelly went around and picked up the lamp, which surprisingly hadn't shattered everywhere, and straightened up the coffee table.

"Sometimes coffee tables just come out of nowhere," Roland quipped, making Nelly smile, despite her concern and fear. What was going on with her grandma?

"That's what happened. It just jumped right out." Her gram sounded a lot more like her old self.

"You didn't hurt yourself, did you, Nelly?" she asked, and Nelly just about fell over.

"You know who I am?" Nelly asked, and while she hated the vulnerability in her voice, she couldn't quite bring herself to be confident.

"Of course. My granddaughter. You're getting home from school. I guess I must have been coming out to greet you, although I kind of blacked out on that part," her gram said. Then she looked up at Roland. "It was awfully nice of you to help me out. I'm not quite the featherweight that I used to be, and I might be a little bit much for Nelly to handle. She needs a good strong man in her life," she said, tapping on Roland's arm like he was the good strong man that she needed.

As if.

There was no way. Now, her Secret Saint partner, on the other hand...

No, she wasn't going to think about that right now. Although, she was still struggling with whether or not it was okay to have feelings and an emotional attachment for someone that she didn't even know. He was obviously a Christian, and he was concerned about pleasing the Lord and living a life that followed what the Bible commanded, not just being a Christian in name only.

Like Roland.

Except...Roland was gently helping her gram over to the recliner and convincing her to sit down for a moment, after she admitted to having a dizzy spell.

"Maybe a glass of water would help?" he asked.

"I suppose I wouldn't mind getting one. Although, why don't you just stay right here, Nelly, and let Roland go grab a glass of water. It's good to see a familiar face," her grandma said.

Nelly hurried over, glad that her gram actually wanted her. She was feeling rather extraneous.

"Is it okay if I get a glass of water from the kitchen?" Roland asked in a low tone that she figured was meant for her ears only as they passed in the living room.

"Of course it is. Thank you," she said, still not quite able to believe that Roland McBride was actually in her living room, helping her, and not mouthing off with a bunch of sarcastic comments and disagreeing with every word that came out of her mouth.

"Are you okay?" she asked her grandmother.

"It was just a little tumble. I didn't even hit the floor. Why are you so worried?" Gram asked.

She didn't know whether to be honest with her gram about her confusion or not. "You didn't recognize me when I walked in the door."

"I didn't? Are you sure? I mean, maybe you had kind of a long day at school, and you're exhausted. Perhaps you should take a nap."

"I think I'm okay," Nelly said slowly. Her grandma didn't have any recollection of being confused. It was like the whole thing didn't happen. She'd totally blocked it out.

"Maybe you should go get a glass of water for yourself. I'll be okay here, and I want to talk to you a bit, but...you're doing a lot. Maybe you're just working a little too hard."

She shook her head, but she did rise to her feet. Maybe she could meet Roland in the kitchen, and...she wasn't sure. But a glass of water didn't sound like a bad idea.

She hurried into the kitchen and met Roland as he shut the spigot off with a full glass in his hand.

"I'm sorry. I didn't mean to kind of make myself at home in your kitchen. I'd opened three cupboard doors before I found the ones with the glasses in them."

"That's not a bother at all. I appreciate you being here. It's... I suppose you were delivering a Christmas tree?" she asked. Roland was not one of her contacts, but maybe he was one of her Secret Saint partner's contacts, since her Secret Saint partner seemed to have no trouble getting Christmas trees when they needed them.

"I was. I heard a crash, and I think you yelped—it wasn't quite a scream. The door was open... I'm sorry I kind of barged in."

"No. I appreciate you making sure. If Grandma had fallen on the floor or needed an ambulance, I just—appreciate the help."

He seemed as amazed as she did that they were actually having a civil conversation for the first time in their lives.

It really was the first time in their lives, and she thought back about it. She couldn't remember them ever talking in a rational way before.

"I don't want to tell you what to do or anything, but I have a little bit of experience with this. My mom's mom lived with us for a while when she had dementia. It was a slowly progressing thing. Has she been checked out by a doctor?"

"No. I need to do that. But...I guess I've been in denial. And the episodes haven't been that many or that long. And it's Christmas."

"Yeah. Everybody's busy at Christmastime. You don't want to

add more to your schedule by shoving in a doctor's appointment somewhere. I totally get it."

"Yeah. But I don't want to put it off."

"Well, the doctor isn't going to be able to do anything to help her. They'll just give you some advice on how to handle things and what to look for and when she's going to start needing full-time care."

"When, not if?" she asked, and there was a part of her that was hoping, truly hoping that he would be able to tell her that once his gram moved in with them, she had gotten better and was better for a long time. But no such luck.

"Yeah. It gets progressively worse. They have a lot of good days and a few bad episodes, and it progresses to where she has good days and bad days, and then she has more bad days than good days, and then she pretty much never knows you."

"Wow. That's depressing."

"It is. I've often wondered why? I mean, why is that the cycle of life, you know?"

"Wow. I've never even thought about it."

"Yeah, I don't know. I guess probably because of Grandma. But why does God allow that? Why don't we just die? Why do we have to suffer and decline for so long?"

"Maybe it gives other people character by taking care of us?"

"Maybe. But we have babies for that, right?"

"True. And we spend our lives trying to grow closer to the Lord and becoming more like Jesus, and then at the end of our lives, we slowly lose all of our abilities and forget who we even are. I just... I don't really get it."

"Yeah."

They were quiet for a while, and Nelly was partially astonished that Roland actually had a spiritual side. He thought about deep questions. Even questions that she hadn't thought about. And he had good answers for them too.

"I guess in the same vein, I've often wondered why when a Christian couple gets married, they become one, right?"

"Right."

"Well then, why does one of them die and the other one doesn't? If they're one, shouldn't they both die together? Why does God want us to spend decades learning to live with someone, to love them despite their faults, to have a sacrificial attitude and love toward them, and have their marriage become like the relationship between Christ and the church, and then one of them dies, and the one that has spent decades trying to not just put up with the other one but love them, all of a sudden they're alone. And they have to learn to be alone. If they were one, shouldn't they die together?"

She had never considered that. And Roland seemed like such a happy-go-lucky kind of person, always laughing, always messing around, or else arguing with her, and giving her a hard time, making fun of her, being sarcastic. The idea that he was capable of such deep thought shocked her.

"I don't have an answer for that. And I guess I have to admit that I've never even really thought about it."

He lifted his shoulder like it wasn't a big deal. "I guess I probably wouldn't have either if it hadn't been for Grandma. But she had been married, and Grandpa died, and that's why she moved in with us. They'd been married for almost sixty years. And you could tell she missed him every single day. She'd grown used to being with him, putting up with everything that he did, and he wasn't really an easy person to get along with if I recall correctly. But she had learned to love him, and she wasn't the same when he passed away. I often wondered, why did she have to spend sixty years putting up with someone, learning to love them anyway, and then God takes them, and she has to learn to be alone again? I just didn't get it."

Nelly couldn't believe that she was actually having a spiritual conversation with Roland. Roland, who was always sarcastic and goofy and funny, and made fun of her and argued with every word that came out of her mouth, actually had a spiritual side that was rather deep, exploring questions she'd never even thought about before.

"I guess I don't have any answers for that."

"I don't either. I suppose it's kind of depressing, and I'm sorry. Although it's something that I wonder about, because either I'll die young, or I'll go through what your grandma is going through. And I've figured out that part of living life well is preparing yourself for the things that you're going to face and then facing them using the Word of God as your guide. I just... I'm not sure how to guide myself through that."

Wow.

"That's really good," she said, feeling lame, after he said so many deep things, and she was just so shocked that she couldn't manage to get anything out of her mouth.

"Anyway, typically staying calm, not arguing with them, and basically letting them do what they want, although giving calm suggestions, but not demanding, works best. Because usually when you demand, they get belligerent and refuse to do absolutely anything that you suggest. It's best if you can kind of guide them and let them think that it's their idea." He held up the glass of water. "But I think the crisis is over for today."

"That's good advice. I'll try to keep that in mind."

Again, Roland was giving her advice, and it was good advice, and he was saying it in a normal tone and talking to her like a normal person. It was weird.

"I'm gonna take this in to your gram," he said, nodding at her.

"I'll be right in. She suggested I get a drink, and I felt like she was right. Thanks for talking to me. I feel better having spoken with you."

He laughed a little. "I don't know how you do. It was kind of deep and dark stuff. I wish... I wish I could say something more encouraging."

Their eyes met for a heavy moment, and communication seemed to flow between them, but she didn't know why. Then he turned and walked into the living room.

She felt like he was sincere. He truly did wish that he could make her happy? Say something nice?

The idea was just so strange. They had been enemies forever, and now all of a sudden, Roland was in her house doing something kind?

Or maybe it was her. Maybe she had just looked at him through the glasses of what she thought he should be, rather than what he was, and just made assumptions about every move he made—mean, unkind, wrong assumptions.

She got a drink and set the glass down on the counter, feeling better.

This would be okay. It would pass, they would get through it. She would have to figure some things out. But she had time. Roland said that there were episodes, and they had good days and bad days... She might have to talk to the family and figure something out for Gram, but it didn't have to happen today.

She walked into the room to see Roland kneeling at her gram's feet, talking to her, with her gram laughing at something he had said.

"There you are. I thought you got lost in the kitchen," Gram said, patting Roland's arm. "This guy has been keeping me entertained with stories from him and his siblings growing up. My goodness, it's been so long since we had children in the house. Wouldn't that be nice?"

"It keeps you young, that's for sure," Roland said, straightening.

"Thanks a lot for helping," Nelly said as she came closer and Roland stepped back.

"No problem. But if you guys are good, I'm gonna head out."

"My goodness, son. You can go if you need to, but just remember, you're welcome here anytime. Especially if you're going to tell a couple of really good stories," Gram said, looking young and happy and like she hadn't had a major episode of confusion and discombobulation just a few minutes ago.

"Yeah. You're welcome back anytime," Nelly said, meeting Roland's gaze directly.

If she was right, she got the feeling that he was just as unsettled about their newfound...truce? Friendship? Kindness toward each other? as she was.

"If there's anything I can do, for either one of you, just let me know, okay?"

He didn't have to say for both of them and include her in his statement. Her grandma was one thing, but she was so surprised that he was offering to help her if she needed it that she barely waved as he turned and strode to the front door, opening it and disappearing.

"My goodness, what a nice young man," her grandma said.

"Isn't he?" Nelly said faintly, hardly able to believe that she was saying such a thing about Roland McBride.

Chapter Sixteen

*R*oland waited by the tree at a quarter till midnight. He couldn't wait to see his partner. They had talked off and on about the people that they worked with and how annoying those people were, but he couldn't believe how good he had felt after he had been kind to Nelly that day.

And there was something about Nelly, something...familiar, or nice or attractive about her, that surprised him. Something he hadn't taken the time to notice before. He'd noticed it especially when he had been talking in the kitchen, mostly talking to try to calm her down and to ease her mind, to give her something to think about— that everything happened for a reason, although he hadn't quite figured out what the reason was, but regardless. He had felt really awesome for the rest of the day. Of course, he had been delivering free Christmas trees to people in town who needed them, and that always made him feel good too.

Regardless, he found himself wanting to pace, anxiously anticipating the arrival of his partner.

She showed up just a few minutes later, more than ten minutes early. He hoped that meant that she couldn't wait to talk to him too.

"Hey there," she said, sounding a little breathless, like she'd been hurrying to get to him.

"Hey. Have a good day?"

"The best. You know the person that I've been telling you about that I've been having such a hard time with?"

"Yeah?" he asked, curious.

"Well, I had a little bit of a breakthrough with that today. Just in my thoughts, and I realized that sometimes you just see someone the way you want to see them, instead of the way they actually are, you know?"

"Wow. That's awesome. That can change your whole perspective."

"It can. And I just had the best day. Anyway, you?"

"I couldn't wait to tell you that I actually had a really great interaction with the person that I have been telling you about. I mean, we're not best friends or anything, but I felt like we connected on a deeper spiritual level than we ever had before. And I took time to listen to them, and they took time to listen to me. And...I guess I wouldn't have said communication is everything, but I think it's attitude and the way you look at things. And yeah, I just had a whole shift today. Isn't that cool that both of us kind of had breakthroughs?"

"I think it's because I've been talking to you, and I've been deliberately trying to make sure that I am thinking about the Lord, trying to do what pleases Him. And trying to look at the world through His eyes. After all, this person that I have so much trouble getting along with is a beloved child of God, and God loves them. I should too."

"That's such a great way to look at it. I don't know if it'll stay, because I'm going to have to work with this person tomorrow." He thought about the Christmas program and the practice that they would need to have. Would he and Nelly be able to get along through that? He wasn't sure. Up until that point, they'd argued at every turn, but hopefully today's interaction with her gram was a turning point.

He thought maybe he'd been able to ease her mind a little bit, and she certainly surprised him by being kind to him, and also...he realized exactly how much she had on her plate. Not just working all day in the classroom, but coming home and taking care of her gram, grading papers, and now spearheading the Christmas play. Of course she was overwhelmed and busy.

He really admired her too, for being willing to take care of her gram. So many people just threw up their hands and placed them in a home.

But Nelly was doing the hard thing—juggling her work and trying to take care of her gram at the same time. He realized that she probably wouldn't be able to continue to do that forever, and he felt a little bit bad for her, which was new. Usually, he just felt annoyed with her.

"I just wanted to thank you for encouraging me to be like Jesus. It's really made a difference in the way that I've been walking through the world. Thank you," he said, feeling like this whole shift that he had with Nelly was completely the result of the interactions he had with his Secret Saint partner.

"I have to say, I've been thinking the same thing. I think the change I had today in a positive direction was because of you. I really appreciate you always encouraging me to live on a higher plane. It's been inspiring. Thank you."

They stood there for a bit, and he didn't know about her, but under his ski mask, he was smiling.

"You really helped me challenge my misconceptions of other people," she said softly. "And not only have I learned to keep my eyes out to watch for things that aren't obvious to everyone—a woodpile that's too low, a porch that needs to be repaired and hasn't been for a while, or just watching as a child opens their lunch from home, and they have a banana and a slice of buttered bread."

"I think we've talked about that before. How doing this has opened my eyes to others, and you've kept me and encouraged me to consider my actions."

"I don't think I've done that on purpose."

"No. But I've watched you and listened to you. You've been very considerate of other people, just knowing what they want or need, and I think that's really important…" He paused. "Sometimes it frustrates me when I see family members not taking care of their family. You know?" He thought about Nelly again, how she was sacrificing to make sure that her grandma had someone taking care of her.

"I know what you mean. Like family members who could, but are too selfish, and choose not to. Or…maybe they just don't get along, and they don't want to make the effort to do something nice for someone that they really don't like."

"Yeah, we can't get past our feelings to do what's right. Isn't that a core principle of Christianity? Not worrying about your feelings, but doing what's right regardless of how you feel."

"It's amazing how people act like their feelings are validated and that because they feel a certain way, it totally negates anything that the Bible teaches."

"I've seen that over and over again, and I've even caught myself doing it at times. I hate to admit that, but it's true." He thought about how he had treated Nelly at times. He had not liked her and so acted like it was okay for him to not be nice, even though the Bible clearly taught that a person should be kind.

"Oh my goodness, I've definitely done the same. And our feelings can be so strong. We just kind of get caught up in a whirlwind of how we feel, and we don't stop to think, 'Is this really the way I want to act?'"

"Yeah, because every day we do things, we are building our reputation. And I've always thought that I want to have a reputation as someone who was levelheaded and kind, but as I look back on my life, I can see why people would think differently, you know?"

"Yeah. We don't stop to think that it's the little moments that build our reputation. I guess somehow we just think that the way we think about ourselves is the way everybody else should think about us too, but if our actions don't say what we want them to, then people aren't going to get the right impression."

"You're right." He hardly ever had this deep of a conversation with anyone, but then he thought about the conversation that he had with Nelly in the kitchen. He actually had talked about things that he hadn't talked about with anyone before. He'd been inspired to say it to try to help her, but she hadn't laughed at him, or rolled her eyes, or acted like someone like him shouldn't be talking about deep spiritual things. Instead...it's almost like she'd been impressed.

He'd certainly been impressed with her.

He and his partner changed the subject and began to talk about things that they could do the next night and laid some plans down for some bigger Secret Saint activities. The closer they got to Christmas, the more they wanted to see how many and how much they could help. It was like they were totally on the same page. It was interesting how God had provided him a partner with whom he was so in tune and so compatible.

He left feeling happy clear down to his soul. Not just because of his interaction with his Secret Saint, although that was a good bit of it. She was perfectly compatible, and he knew that his feelings for her were deepening, even though he really didn't know who she was or anything else about her. He did know her heart was pure. And he thought it was probably okay to continue working with her, even though he was skating dangerously close to being emotionally involved and attached.

What was the worst that could happen?

But he also felt good because of what had happened with Nelly that day. Instead of being unkind and sarcastic, the way he usually was, he'd done something nice, and it had made him feel so much better about himself and the world in general.

And on top of that, Nelly had responded in kind, reflecting the way he had acted. So maybe, maybe instead of all of those years of competition, if he had just been kind, maybe she would have responded in a good way, and their years of constantly trying to one-up the other would have never happened. Maybe they would even have been...friends.

Chapter Seventeen

Nelly arrived early and parked at the church.

She'd been so excited about all the good things that had happened yesterday that she hadn't slept very well. Not during her nap before she got up at midnight to go meet her Secret Saint partner, nor when she got back.

Her alarm had gone off seemingly way too early, and while her gram hadn't had any more confused episodes, her concern and worry over that had also been keeping her up.

Still, she was looking forward to working with the children, especially since the previous day's rehearsal had been cancelled because of a school practice that many of the children were involved in. They had a few new faces and were almost sure to have guests who had never been in church before attending the program.

Anything that Nelly could do to help spread the gospel was always a blessing, and she wanted to put her very best in.

She was a few minutes early, and the kids were playing in the downstairs rec room as she walked in.

Pastor Connelly looked up as she walked in, his face grave.

He started to walk over toward her, and Nelly felt a ball forming in her stomach. What in the world could he want? He didn't look happy.

"Can I talk to you for a minute?" he asked as he stood in front of her, forgoing any kind of pleasant greeting.

"Of course," she said, adjusting her bag over her shoulder and following him to the stairwell, closing the door behind them.

The stairs led up to the sanctuary, but he stood at the landing at the bottom.

"Do you remember how we had discussed how we weren't getting as many donations as we normally do?"

"Yes?"

"Yeah. Well, the church is never locked, and I thought that maybe someone could be taking it, so I decided that in the morning when I came to my office, I would count the money in the box and then count it again in the evening just to see if anyone was actually taking money. Well, Monday nothing happened, but Tuesday... We lost almost one hundred dollars out of the box."

"You're kidding!" Nelly said, unable to believe that someone would take that much. It was one thing to maybe swipe a dollar, but wow.

Again, the pastor's face held no sign of humor, or even a smile, as he shook his head. His mouth flattened as he glanced around before lowering his voice. "I think that it might be Roland who is stealing it."

"What?" she said, unable to believe her ears. The idea that anyone would think that Roland McBride would steal—it was crazy. Of course, he hadn't been her favorite person in her life, but she had never thought he was actually a thief.

"He was here bringing the tree that the church is going to decorate. He was the only one I saw on the camera. It had to have been him." The pastor's voice was low, his tone dead serious.

"I'm sorry, I just don't believe for one second that Roland McBride—I know we've had our differences over the years, but there is absolutely no way that he would ever touch the church's money. In fact, he was trying to tell you that it was there and vulnerable. Why would he have done that if he was the one stealing it?"

"Because he was just getting that idea in his head, and then...he decided to act on it. I don't know why people do the things that they do. But I'm telling you, it had to have been him."

"And I'm telling you, I've known Roland McBride since before we were both in school. We were in the church nursery together, for goodness' sake. That man would never steal anything."

The pastor looked at her for a moment and then lifted his shoulder. "Well, I am going to file a police report, and in my opinion, Roland is the top suspect. I thought that you might corroborate that story."

"Absolutely not. There's no way that I could ever implicate him in that. I know—I am absolutely sure down to my soul that it was not him." She knew her voice was loud, and she tried to modulate it some, but even though she and Roland had never considered themselves friends, she absolutely was sure that he would never do anything like that. For a moment, she stopped to question herself. How was she so sure? Why did she have this really strong feeling that it absolutely could not be Roland?

She thought about the misconceptions that she had about him, how she thought for years that he was just not a good person. And she realized that, even though she thought that, deep down, she knew that he was upright and honest. And when challenged by it, she could say with certainty that he just wasn't that type of man.

"I don't think that you ought to—I think it's perfectly okay to file a report, but I wouldn't implicate him. I'm telling you, he might be the only person on the video, but he is absolutely innocent."

"I'm going to have to tell them what I think. And then it'll be up to them to make a decision. I'm not the police. I'm just the person who saw Roland on the video."

"He was delivering a tree. He was donating it. Giving something to the church."

"Maybe he took that hundred dollars as payment."

"Roland would never do that. I'm sure of it." She felt like she was fighting a losing battle. She had no evidence that Roland didn't do it, but he had absolutely no evidence, other than Roland donating a tree to the church, that he would have. It frustrated her to think that just because he was on camera, he was guilty. After all, how could he donate a tree without actually coming to the church and giving it to them?

"Thanks for your time," Pastor Connelly said.

Nelly gritted her teeth, but she knew she needed to get back out there. Roland was probably there right now and wondering why she wasn't.

She turned to go and looked up at the stairs. Roland stood at the top.

Chapter Eighteen

oland stood at the top of the stairs, shocked.

Not just shocked because Pastor Connelly would actually think that he would steal money, although he was, but he was flabbergasted that Nelly was defending him and so vehemently. She was absolutely sure that he did not take the money.

That was crazy. Why would she come to his defense so ardently?

He wasn't sure what to make of it, but it made his heart feel funny in a way that he couldn't ever remember it feeling before.

"Roland," she said, her eyes widening, shock in her voice.

"Hey. I… The parking lot was full, so I parked up here."

He didn't mean to eavesdrop on their conversation, but when the pastor looked at Nelly with a knowing look in his eyes, he realized that the pastor thought he was coming up through here to possibly scope out the money situation again.

Nelly narrowed her eyes at the pastor, shook her head, and then opened the door and walked out.

It closed with a click behind her as Roland slowly started walking down the stairs.

"I guess I couldn't help but hear that," Roland said. There was no point in trying to avoid it. Obviously the pastor thought he was guilty, and even Nelly's fierce defense of him was not convincing him otherwise.

"I'm sorry, Roland. I really hate to think this way, but...you're the only one on the camera. There's just no way that it couldn't be you."

"I guess you have to think what you have to think. But...for what it's worth, Nelly is right. There's no way in the world I would ever take any money from the church. Ever. I don't even think I would let you give it to me. I would have to be desperate. My goal is to serve, not to steal or even to be served."

"There's a time and a place for everyone to be served. After all, other people can't serve if you're not willing to be served. But that's a sermon for a different day. I just... I can't square it any other way. The video would have caught anyone else coming and going, and it didn't. You were the only one."

"Do you have cameras on all of the doors?"

"The camera shows the entire front porch."

"Maybe someone came in the bottom door and up the stairs."

"Interestingly, we typically have the bottom door locked. I'm not sure why, but that's just the way it was done before I came. So I don't argue with the ladies in charge. I know my place."

The pastor seemed to be trying to make a little bit of a joke, but Roland didn't feel like laughing. He was being accused of an extremely odious crime, and while he appreciated the fact that Nelly considered him innocent, and he hoped that that was the way the rest of the townspeople felt, he remembered what he had said to his Secret Saint partner. His actions hadn't always been the actions of the person he wanted to be thought of as. In other words, it would not be a total stretch of the imagination for many people in town to think that it could have been him, because while he had absolutely never stolen anything or done anything of the sort, he did have a reputation for being not kind, at least where Nelly was concerned. And he supposed people could say he wasn't completely responsible—he could remember a few times throughout the years where he did not uphold his end of bargains he had made.

Since he'd hit his mid-twenties and matured, he had not acted terribly at all, but sometimes small towns had long memories.

"Unfortunately I'm going to have to report it. The money is not mine. I'm just a representative of the church. And I've got to tell the police what is going on, and...your name is going to come up, because it's you on the video."

"I know. I was here. You're right. I set up the tree in the sanctuary."

Pastor Connelly nodded, and they stood there in silence for just a bit, and then Roland said, "I need to go. Nelly is expecting my help, and it's past time to start."

The pastor nodded again and opened the door, allowing Roland to walk through first.

He didn't feel very good—there was a heaviness in his soul that he hated. But there wasn't anything he could do about it. Pastor Connelly had to say what he had to say, and whatever happened would happen. But they would never be able to prove that he took the money, because he absolutely did not.

To his surprise, Nelly did not have the children lined up and had not begun practice. Instead, she and Mrs. Tucker were talking by the door.

Roland almost went to begin to get things rolling, but instead, he turned and walked toward the two ladies who were speaking. Nelly looked concerned, and that made Roland's stomach turn over. What else could be happening?

"I don't know what they're going to do. They don't meet until tomorrow, and tomorrow evening is the tree lighting ceremony! How can we light a tree that is missing!"

"What tree is missing?" Roland asked as he walked up to the two ladies. Mrs. Tucker looked extremely agitated.

"The tree at the center of the town square. The one that we were all supposed to finish decorating and light tomorrow. Apparently it was stolen sometime today. Nobody really knows when. The thief must have taken it in broad daylight."

"That would not be an easy tree to steal. It's huge. It must be nine feet tall." They had donated it from their tree farm, but by the time it had been cut and re-stood, he wasn't sure exactly how tall it was.

"Well, they did it. Maybe with a truck."

"I don't think there are any cameras on the town square. I guess... normally there's nothing to steal there."

"Yes, I already checked. There are no cameras. And like I said, we're not going to be able to solve anything until tomorrow morning, and how would we be able to get a tree that fast?"

Roland wasn't worried about it. He could leave a note for the Secret Saint after he left the Christmas program practice. He could let her know that they needed to postpone the deliveries that they were planning on making tonight and instead go to the tree farm, grab a tree, and get it stood up again.

"Didn't it already have lights on it?" Roland asked.

"They stole it, lights and all," Mrs. Tucker said, snapping her mouth closed and looking disgusted.

"Wow. So that was probably five or six strands of lights."

"It was ten. Ten strands of lights and a nine-foot-tall Christmas tree. Who in the world would think of stealing something like that? And what in the world would they do with it?" Mrs. Tucker sounded like the world was about to come to an end.

"Well, obviously, it was someone who wanted to spread Christmas cheer somewhere else," Roland said. He was starting to feel a little bit better. Nothing was ever as bad as it seemed at first, and even if he was accused of stealing the money, they couldn't prove it, and...his reputation would take a hit, because some people would never forget that he had been accused, even though no proof was ever presented. Still, God had a reason for all of this, and the best thing that he could do was to not worry about it and just trust that God was going to work it all out for his good and God's glory. After all, he said he wanted to live for God's glory, but…so many times he found himself wanting to live for his own. Like his reputation. He didn't want it to be shredded, but if it happened, through no fault of his own, then God promised that He would work it out.

He had been able to reason that through in his head, and while it still bothered him, because of course he wanted to have a good reputation, he had to say that he trusted God more than he trusted himself, and he just needed to let go and believe.

"All right. The idea that someone would stoop so low as to steal a town Christmas tree is disturbing, but there's nothing we can do about it now, and we need to work on the Christmas program."

Nelly looked up at Roland. "Are you okay?" she asked, and his heart stirred. She was concerned about him? She had heard the accusations, she had defended him more fiercely than his family probably would, and now she was asking if he was okay. Wow. It made him feel good in a way he couldn't explain.

"I'm fine."

She nodded. She opened her mouth like she was going to say something else, and then she closed it. Maybe because Mrs. Tucker was standing there, or maybe because she didn't want to get too touchy-feely with him, he wasn't sure.

But he got the impression that she was going to say that she believed he was innocent.

The Christmas practice went well, and while there still was a bit of an undercurrent between the two of them, they got along much better than they had before. He almost enjoyed working with her. It certainly didn't have the fun and easy camaraderie that working with his Secret Saint partner did, but it wasn't bad. Honestly.

He left practice a little early, saying that he needed to get home to his mother, which wasn't entirely untrue. He wrote out a note explaining what was going on and hoped that his Secret Saint partner would still check the tree for notes as he tucked it inside. They hadn't left too many, but this was one of those things where he needed to contact her. He was pretty sure she would agree that the tree took precedence. After all, the entire town turned out for the tree lighting ceremony, and the businesses relied on the income they made to pad their bottom line and stay profitable.

There was no one around when he stopped and got out, ran to the tree, and tucked his note inside. He still didn't see anyone as he walked back and got back in his pickup.

It was the first time they had changed plans, and hopefully his partner would go along with it.

Chapter Nineteen

Nelly's step was light as she walked toward their meeting spot at twenty till midnight.

She had gotten the note out of the tree as she was about to put her own note in. She had been impressed. His sources were really good, although she supposed that one only had to drive down Main Street in order to see that the Christmas tree was missing.

Still, she had no idea where he lived, and if he lived out of town, for him to have figured it out in less than twelve hours was pretty amazing in her opinion.

Regardless, she was all in about skipping out on their earlier plans and focusing on the tree. After all, not only was it something to do for the town, but she loved the annual Christmas tree lighting celebration, and she didn't want anything to mess it up.

Hopefully the police would figure out who had taken the tree and the money. Maybe the same person had done both.

And surely no one was going to accuse Roland of stealing the very tree he had donated to the town square.

That kind of cast a pall over everything for her. She couldn't believe that the pastor would believe that Roland could do such a thing, and it bothered her. She wanted to figure out some way of exonerating his name.

Interestingly, Roland didn't seem to be too bothered by it. At least he hadn't acted like it had while they were doing the Christmas program with the children. He had been helpful and encouraging and patient the way he always was. And he hadn't even snipped and snapped at her like he usually did. Typically, there was an underlying tension, a push and pull back and forth, that they both made sure not to allow to erupt in front of the children, but both of them knew they wanted to. Sometimes there were angry glares and narrow eyes as well. But all of that had been missing today.

Was it because he had heard her defend him?

Nothing else had changed.

It didn't matter—she felt good for saying what she knew was right. There had to be another explanation. Maybe the camera blanked out, or maybe someone had cut a wire like what happened in the movies. She didn't know; she just knew that it couldn't be Roland.

"Good evening," she said as her Secret Saint partner stepped out from the shadows. She was twenty minutes early, and her partner was already there. It made her smile—she loved that he was dependable and conscientious about his work.

"I'm sorry about the change of plans." He spoke immediately.

"No. I'm happy about them. I am super thrilled that people will wake up in the morning and see that there's a tree, and nothing has to be canceled."

"Yeah. The Christmas tree lighting ceremony is one of my favorite things about Christmas."

"Mine too," she said, shocked that he would admit it. And then, the thought went through her head—her Secret Saint partner would be at the Christmas tree lighting ceremony.

Wow. That made her anticipate it even more. She could look around, try to see if she could find someone who was the same size and stature as him?

No. She didn't want to know his identity, but the idea that he would be there filled her with warmth and anticipation.

"I have my truck parked closer to the town square. I've got a tree in the back and a stand to go with it."

"That's great. I brought fifteen strands of lights. I heard that there were ten, and I wanted to be safe rather than sorry."

"All right then. I've got a ladder in my truck too, so we should be good to go."

"Awesome."

They walked together side by side, toward the town square. She adjusted her cape to make sure it didn't fall down, and he put a hand on his ski mask, as though to make sure it was still there.

"How was your day?" she asked casually as they strolled. It almost felt like they were just out for an evening walk together. She almost wanted to reach over and thread her fingers through his.

Except...that would be entirely inappropriate. She didn't even know who he was.

"I actually had a really good day. I mean, not every day is perfect, and...I suppose something happened that could have ruined it. But it didn't. You know how bad things sometimes become good things?"

"Yeah. I know what you mean." She didn't really have anything like that right now, but it was like God gave them something that could totally derail them, but if they just waited, patiently, with their hand in His, He turned things around.

"Yeah, well, that's kind of what happened. Something that could have been really bad, and then...someone else made it so that, even though they didn't take the problem away, they made it better," he said, his voice kind of trailing off like that wasn't exactly what he wanted to say, but he wasn't exactly sure how to say it.

"That's perfect for around this time of year. Christmas is definitely not a season where we want to wallow in all the bad and evil."

"No. That's why I was so interested in getting this tree back up. We can sit and mope about the fact that we've got a thief among us, or we can just get to work and pull together, and the camaraderie of the community coming together kind of outshines the fact that sometimes there are people who ruin things by displaying a complete and total lack of character."

She laughed. That was one way to put it anyway. "I think, most of the time, the good outweighs the bad. It's just that the bad looms so large in our heads."

"No, I agree. For some reason, it does, but I do think that the good definitely outweighs the bad. Always."

It took a little wrangling from them to get the tree in position, but it helped that the tree was wrapped. It was much easier to put in a stand that way. And her Secret Saint partner was obviously very familiar with handling Christmas trees. She assumed that he had put a lot of Christmas trees up for people, either as a Secret Saint, or as himself, or both.

Part of her brain wanted to go down that trail, thinking about people in town who would have had a reason to put a lot of trees up. But she didn't allow it to do so.

Finally, they decided the tree looked straight from all angles, and her partner took his pocketknife out and cut the wrapping off.

The branches burst out, full and beautiful and perfect.

She walked over to where she had set the bags of lights down and got the first bag out.

"Do we start at the top or the bottom?" she asked.

"My mom always started at the bottom, but I don't know that that is the way the rest of the world does it."

She laughed. "All right. That's where we always started too, although for the last decade, we've had a pre-lit tree, and I haven't had to string lights at all."

"You haven't strung lights at Christmas? Isn't that what Christmas is all about?"

She laughed out loud, because she knew that wasn't what he truly believed. "I guess I've missed the real meaning of the season for at least a decade."

"I'm glad I can give it back to you. My goodness, the idea of not stringing lights on a tree. That's insane."

They shared easy laughter as he removed his gloves, and she did as well. Then, he grabbed the end of the lights and plugged it in. They lit up, and he carefully moved the branches and pushed the plug in next to the trunk, so it wouldn't be so obvious.

She walked around the other side of the tree so he could hand the lights to her as they came around.

She hadn't given much thought to the fact that both of them had taken their gloves off, until he handed her the lights and their fingers brushed. It was unexpected, and she was grateful for her hood that kept her face shielded, since her mouth opened in surprise.

She had not been expecting that, and…it felt odd.

She was careful when she handed them back not to allow it to happen again. Not because she didn't want to, just because…she didn't even know him. She supposed he could be married, but she rejected that idea immediately. He was a man of principle and character, and if he were married, he wouldn't have said he wasn't back when they'd first met.

Not to mention, didn't he say something about maybe giving it up when he got married and had children?

She couldn't remember exactly what they had said about that.

She didn't want those thoughts to intrude anyway and bring down her evening. She'd been having such a great day, despite the shadow that hung over her because of the accusations against Roland.

She had a good mind to ask her partner about it. But so far, she hadn't mentioned any names, and if the pastor went to the police with his accusations, her Secret Saint partner would know exactly who she was talking about and potentially be able to figure out her identity.

She was less concerned about that than she ever had been, but she still wanted to protect it. It was just better that way for everyone.

"So tell me about your family," she said casually as she took the lights from him again and carefully arranged them on the branches in front of her.

"Well," he paused, and she realized what she had said.

"No names. Or identifying information. I wasn't trying to figure out who you were, I was just..." She paused. She might as well just say the truth. "I know you said you weren't married, but...I guess I'm just curious about you."

"There's no way I would be running around with another woman in the middle of the night if I were married to someone. She would be my partner. In fact, I feel like that's what you should be looking for in a partner—someone that you love doing things with. They don't have to be exactly like you, and you don't have to agree on everything."

"I agree with that. You definitely want to be with someone who makes you laugh and who has fun with you, but the most important thing is that they're a Christian."

"A Christian who lives what they believe and doesn't just say it."

"Okay. That's right. I suppose we use the word Christian loosely a lot of times."

"Yeah. But anyway, I guess you know, opposites attract, and you and I have found that our different interests and areas of expertise have given us a really great partnership. I feel like that's what a marriage is. A really great partnership. Where maybe you're the same, like two college professors—they're both kind of boring to the rest of the world, where they sit in their library at night with their noses in books or dissertations or whatever, and they're both completely happy."

"Or that same college professor could be happily married to a man who isn't interested in books or learning, but is good with his hands, and does a lot of handwork around the house, while she maybe runs the finances and takes care of the taxes and that type of thing."

"Yeah. The two college professors would probably be pretty

happy with each other, but they'd have to hire out for a lot of work, because they have the same strengths."

"And there's nothing wrong with that, but you can complement each other and have the same strengths, or you can complement each other and have different strengths. It's probably six of one, half a dozen of the other."

They had to pause for a moment while Nelly grabbed another string of lights, pulled it out of the package, and plugged it into the end of the other one.

She took a little bit of time to make sure that she had that end tucked in amongst the branches before she started to unwind it again.

"So you don't have to be exactly the same, but you do have to have some shared interests or shared something."

"Yeah. Probably a college professor and…who wouldn't be compatible with a college professor?"

"Someone who is in a motorcycle gang?" She shrugged her shoulders. "I don't even know. I guess they still could end up together, you know? You expand another person's world when you're not exactly like them. And as long as you're willing to have your world expanded—"

"And as long as it's not being expanded away from the Lord," he interrupted her.

"Exactly. But just someone who shows you life beyond what you know. And that's a good partnership, I think."

"So you're saying you're looking for someone who doesn't live in Mistletoe Meadows?"

She laughed. "No. Not at all. I mean, I guess I don't care, and I don't think I would mind being married to someone who wasn't from here. But it'd be nice to be married to someone who knows and loves the same things I do."

"So you do think it's better to have someone who's exactly like you?" he said, like he had a gotcha moment with her.

"No. I would be just as happy being married to someone who

didn't, as long as we shared the most important things. And as long as... I don't know, I guess you could really be married to anyone as long as they loved the Lord and followed Him."

"That's the conclusion that I've come to. I mean, I haven't thought about it a whole lot, but it doesn't really matter whether they're from here, or there, or across the world, or whether they're my complete, total opposite."

"With that said, arranged marriages should be okay then."

"I don't know if I'd go that far," he said.

They laughed and continued to chat, the feeling of camaraderie and working together warming her heart as it always did when she was with her partner.

All too soon, they were done, and they parted ways, heading back to their respective homes. For some reason, her heart was a lot lighter. Whether it was because she now knew that he was truly unmarried, or whether it was...just the joy of doing wonderful things with someone she admired and respected, she wasn't sure. But becoming a Secret Saint was one of the best things she'd done in a long time.

Chapter Twenty

Today was one of Roland's favorite days of the year—the community Christmas tree lighting ceremony.

Roland loved that he had been able to, with the help of his Secret Saint partner, get another tree, so none of the festivities had to be canceled.

"I don't know who got this tree, but it's pretty amazing."

He smiled to himself as he overhead one woman talking to another as they passed him on the sidewalk.

"I think it was the work of the Secret Saint," another older lady said as they stopped in front of him. He was adjusting the ladder, since he would be hanging decorations from the top of the tree.

Judd had a ladder and was going to do the other side.

There were various people below with boxes of ornaments, and someone would be handing things up to him.

He knew his partner was around here somewhere, and while he wanted to kind of keep an eye out for her, to try to figure out who she was, most of him wanted to just stay anonymous. He wouldn't appreciate it if she were trying to figure him out, although...maybe there was a part of him that wouldn't mind.

Regardless, he kept his mind on getting up the ladder without tipping it over, and making sure it was sturdy at the bottom.

He noticed Nelly Bushnell with a box of ornaments in her hand.

She had started to put them up on the bottom of the tree when Mrs. Tucker came over to her, her hand out, hurrying as though Nelly were going to ruin everything if she put an ornament in the wrong spot.

"No! You cannot put those small ornaments there. They belong at the top. Here, come over here and hand them up to Roland. Roland, make sure that you arrange these not too close to each other, but all the small ones go at the top."

Mrs. Tucker bustled away without saying anything else.

Maybe it was his imagination, but she seemed to have given him a side glance, almost as though she was afraid that he was going to walk off with the ornaments or something, like she believed he walked off with the money at the church.

He heard whispers around town, and honestly, there was a small, very small, part of him that had considered not coming today. But that would have made it look like he was guilty, and he was not.

"I'm sorry. I guess I've been volunteered to work with you," Nelly said, shrugging her shoulder. "You would think I bother you enough at the Christmas program practice."

"You're not bothering me. I actually don't mind working with you at all," he said. And he realized that was true. The last Christmas program practice had not gone badly, and he actually might have been looking forward to the next one, to his surprise.

"Your mother is looking a little peaked—is she okay?" Nelly said as she came close, lifting a bulb to him.

He paused as he took the bulb from her. "Do you think so?"

She seemed a little surprised at the intensity of his question, and her eyes widened before she looked across at where his mother was sitting down, drinking hot chocolate and talking to the mayor's wife.

"Yeah, I guess. She just always has been in the thick of everything before, and today she's sitting down. Just seems odd."

"I keep telling my siblings something's wrong, and I keep asking Mom if she wants to make a doctor's appointment, and everybody keeps stonewalling me. It's a little vindicating to hear that you at least noticed."

"Well, I guess if your siblings think she's okay and your mom won't go to the doctor anyway, there's not much you can do."

"No. There's not, but it does seem nice to have someone else noticing what I've been noticing for the last several weeks."

They didn't say anything else as he took the bulb from her hands and hung it on the tree.

"Do you think this will satisfy Mrs. Tucker?" he asked, knowing it was unnecessary.

"I don't know, I think I would move it over to the left a little bit," she said, and he looked at the branch, realizing that there was nothing but air to the left of the bulb, and then he looked down at her and saw her eyes twinkling.

Nelly Bushnell was teasing him.

He laughed. "I don't know. Do you think it'll look good hanging in midair?" he asked, pretending to consider the idea.

"I don't know. You're a magician—you can do it, right?" She grinned. And for just a second, he wondered if she knew that he was the Secret Saint.

Then he dismissed that as a possibility and thought he was just being paranoid.

"I don't think anyone, magician or no, could satisfy Mrs. Tucker."

"I agree with you. Because I think that group includes the late Mr. Tucker, who never seemed to be able to do anything right, although I'm holding out hope that eventually she will amend her ways and be satisfied with the sincere effort that people put in, instead of insisting that nothing is correct unless it is done entirely her way to her specifications."

He smiled. Nelly wasn't saying anything unkind—she was just pointing out that some people needed to have everything done their way and never really learned to compromise. Probably if Mr. Tucker had had a spine and said no to his wife once in a while, she wouldn't be the way she was. Or maybe it was her parents... Or maybe it was just her, needing to teach herself that kindness was more important than perfection.

"So, I think we just found something we agree on."

"Mrs. Tucker?" Nelly said as she handed up another ornament.

"No. That kindness is more important than perfection."

"Oh my goodness. This is getting dangerous. You and me, getting along? Agreeing?"

"You defending me?" he said, his voice slow, and maybe there was a little extra emotion in his gaze.

He thought maybe he was being too vulnerable, because she paused, an ornament dangling midair between her two fingers.

He dropped his gaze to her hand, noticing the slenderness of her fingers and the delicate translucence of her skin.

Her nails were tapered, and she held the bulb gently but firmly. While her fingers looked delicate, they also seemed capable.

Maybe he was focusing on her fingers to keep from focusing on their conversation.

"You know, we had a pretty good competition going for a lot of years, and maybe it turned into something a little bit more than what I had intended, or...maybe I was just hurt and it always came out, but I never thought you were a bad person. Ever. And I didn't say anything to Pastor Connelly that wasn't absolutely true," Nelly finally said, and sometime as she spoke, his eyes went to hers again.

"I appreciated it." At the time, he'd wondered if he would have been as ardent a defender of her as she had been of him. He'd like to think he would have been, but he wasn't entirely sure. She had defended him like he was her brother or husband, like she knew him better than she actually did or...just believed in him. It was something that made his heart, his whole soul, feel amazing, to think that she would stand up to the pastor of all people to defend his good name.

"Well, I appreciate it," he said, taking the bulb from her and hanging it on the tree.

Soft snowflakes had begun to fall, and they shimmered and glittered in the lights that hung around the tree, and they talked about the weather, and whether they would have a white Christmas, and light topics like that, but underneath there was a bond between them that hadn't been there before.

He finished hanging the bulbs and got off the ladder, and soon the decorating was done, and people congregated around, admiring how beautiful the town square looked, holding steaming cups of hot chocolate, and watching the snow glitter down.

As was custom, Bernard had brought his guitar, and soon they were singing Christmas carols.

Somehow, Roland had ended up not that far from Nelly, and as her voice lifted in harmony with his, their eyes met.

The harmony was unexpected. He certainly wouldn't have expected someone that he had not cared for his entire life to have a voice that blended so well with his, but as they sang the familiar Christmas hymn, there was no doubt that they sounded good together.

She gave a little smile, and he returned it with a full-on grin, never breaking from the notes they sang.

He was pretty sure that he and Nelly were officially friends. And that was the most unusual thing that had happened all year.

Chapter Twenty-One

The evening of the tree lighting ceremony, Nelly worked with her Secret Saint partner, delivering Christmas gifts that had been bought and wrapped by their various contacts to a family who had just lost their grandmother.

She and her partner were talking and laughing softly as they walked through the yard, under an old oak tree with a low-hanging branch. They both ducked as they walked underneath it.

She saw out of the corner of her eye something move quickly, and she turned her head in time to see her partner's hat go flying off his head. It must have caught on the branch, and he continued to walk.

Without thinking about it, she flipped her head around immediately so that she was looking away, even though she stopped.

She heard him gasp, set his box down, and stop.

There was some rustling, and then he said, "I've got it back on."

"That was close," she said as she turned to look at him, realizing it could have been her with the branch catching on her cape and pulling it back as she walked.

"It was awfully nice of you to turn your head. I... I'm impressed at your quick thinking. And at your dedication to making sure that we remain anonymous."

"I've considered asking if we could confess our identities to each other, but...I think it's important that we don't."

"Same. Actually, I've come to the same conclusion. As curious as I am, as much as I'd like to know, I think it's more important that we just keep it a secret. If we can."

"Oh, I think we can. I was tempted to look around earlier this evening at the tree lighting ceremony and see if I could find you, but I didn't want to, even though I did, if that makes sense?"

She'd always made sure to disguise her voice just a little bit as she conversed as the Secret Saint with him. And she assumed that he did too, although she really didn't know. Maybe if she heard his voice when he was wearing his regular clothes, she would recognize it, but part of her hoped not.

"It's just—if I know who you are, and someone asks me, I might be tempted to tell them. Or it might slip somehow." She thought of all the different people that he talked to and how it would be almost impossible to keep a secret like that away from everyone, once it came out.

"Yeah. Exactly. There's just too much chance that someone might accidentally or unintentionally let it slip, so if I don't know, that's one less thing I have to worry about keeping a secret. We're already doing so much and trying to keep it below the radar."

"That's part of what makes it fun. And honestly, I do actually like the idea that we don't know who each other is."

Except for the fact that she was attracted to him and felt like perhaps they would be good together in real life, as well as in Secret Saint activities.

She was a little shaken by the near miss, and as they continued to work, she was very careful to duck so that her hood did not catch on any of the branches in the yard.

They finished up for the night and bid each other a good evening.

Normally Nelly walked away with a really happy feeling in her heart, and she did again that evening, but she also felt a little bit of uncomfortableness. It had been a close call, and that would have upset everything. There was also a little bit of disappointment. It would have been nice to find out his identity. She had to admit that, even as she recoiled at the idea.

It was a complication she hadn't been expecting, and her emotions were jumbled up in a knot, feeling uncomfortable and weird. It was a while before she finally fell asleep that night.

Chapter Twenty-Two

"I've got it, Mom. You go on in," Roland said as his mom made her way to the back of the car where he was opening the door and getting the casserole out.

"Oh, I don't want you to carry all of that," his mom said, but she sounded tired.

He wasn't quite sure why she would be tired, because she had slept all afternoon from what he could figure. He had been out working at the tree farm, and now, since it was Friday night and time for their normal family dinner, their hired guy was holding down the Christmas tree sales.

"Mom, that's why you brought me."

"Oh, Roland. That's not why." His mom laughed, but it also sounded tired to him.

At least she should be able to be perky for the family. Although, he kind of wished she wouldn't be, so they could see a glimpse of what he'd been seeing for the past several weeks, almost a month now.

They walked to the porch, with his mother commenting about

the Christmas lights that they had strung up on it and how pretty the tree looked from the window.

He thought he felt a few drops of sleet coming down and thought about his rendezvous with his partner tonight. They would just be talking about what they were going to do tomorrow night, and he honestly was looking forward to it.

"I'll get the door, Mom," he said, reaching out to grab it so she didn't have to.

She allowed him to open the door, and they stepped through, calling out to the house to let them know they'd arrived.

Summer hurried forward.

"Mom! It's so nice to see you," she said, coming in and giving her a big hug. "Here, I can take that." She offered to take the casserole out of Roland's hands.

He figured she could put it somewhere, and he allowed her to take it, holding onto the bag of potato chips that his mom had brought as well.

It wasn't like her to bring something that wasn't homemade.

"What's that?" Summer asked as the bag crinkled when she took the casserole.

"Oh, I just—I saw those potato chips in the store, and I thought about how much the family would enjoy them," his mom said, and he thought maybe Summer did a double take.

She hadn't been in the family since birth, as he had, but surely she knew how odd that was.

Gilbert came out next, and he held his hand out for the bag.

"Little bro brought chips? That's a shortcut," he said with a laugh after he had given their mom a perfunctory hug.

"Those aren't mine, those are Mom's," Roland said, waiting for his brother's reaction.

"Mom, you got them on sale, huh?" That was not the reaction he was looking for, but he gave a mental shrug. Maybe he really was just imagining it.

"Come to the kitchen and give me a hand if you want to," Summer said to his mom with a grin, knowing that she would go.

"Well, thanks. I think I'll go to the table and sit down though. I want to make sure to get a good seat." She tried to sound chipper, but it wasn't hard for Roland to hear the exhaustion in her voice.

That stopped both Gilbert and Summer in their tracks.

Terry and Judd had been coming out of the hall, and they stopped as well.

Amy had been walking in from the dining room, holding the hand of one of the girls, and she stopped with her mouth open. Jones ran into her and said, "What are you doing?" before he too fell silent, although it was obvious he didn't know what they were all shocked about.

"I think you might have been right about Mom," Judd said slowly.

"Yeah," Amy agreed immediately.

"What did I miss?" Jones said.

"We can talk about it at the table," Summer said, giving everyone a warning glance.

There was a lot of murmuring and talking under one's breath rather than the normal hustle and bustle and laughter that accompanied these meals.

As the food prep was finished and casseroles and containers were set on the table, everyone filed in, and there was a solemn air that had never been there before.

Roland felt rather justified but also a little bit scared.

His mom was a rock. She had always been there for the kids, and the idea that there might be something wrong scared him to death. They were used to looking to her for her wisdom and her calm and wise advice. What would they do without her?

He knew he was jumping the gun. Maybe she had just been fighting the flu for a while, or maybe it was just something else. Something benign, something that she would be over in a month or two. Or maybe it was something worse.

They prayed and passed the food around, and then as people began to eat, Judd spoke from the head of the table.

"Mom," he said, calling her "mom," even though technically she was his wife's mother.

"I don't know what you guys are all upset about," his mom finally said, admitting that there had been an undercurrent—she had known and heard the whispers and conversations that had gone on before everyone got to the table.

"Mother. You have never in your life sat down when there was work to do. You certainly would never allow us to just do it ourselves. What's going on?" Terry asked, her voice heavy with concern.

"Am I not allowed to be a little bit tired?"

The table was quiet. Of course she was allowed to be a little tired. This is when Roland decided that he might be betraying his mother, but he needed to speak up.

"You slept all afternoon. I thought it was because you wanted to be chipper when you got here."

His mother gave him an annoyed look. But he wasn't fooled. He wasn't in trouble.

"That's exactly why I took a nap."

"So you would have energy to help in the kitchen," Gilbert said.

"Yes."

"And then you decided that you'd rather sit at the table than help in the kitchen, even though you took a nap in order to be able to do that," Isadora said. She looked a little discombobulated as well. Her world had already been upset by her husband leaving, and she was getting used to being a single mom. Now, to have something happen to her mom—Roland could only imagine that she did not need her world rocked in that way. Not this soon anyway.

But sometimes a person just didn't get to choose when they were going to go through a trial.

"Guys, I'm fine. This is just the time of year when everyone's tired. You guys are all tired too."

"But we didn't sleep all day and then go in and sit down."

"Isn't an old lady allowed to sit down for a little bit?"

"Mom. I'd really like it if you'd talk to us about this. I think maybe you're due for a checkup." Terry spoke, and while she didn't exactly have her doctor hat on, she had a bit of authority in her tone that even her mother respected.

"Fine. Do you know when I could get in to see the doctor?" she asked, putting a polite smile on her face.

"Anytime, Mom. Come in tomorrow. I'll pick you up on my way there."

"And I can bring you home when you're done," Roland said immediately. He would be out late with his Secret Saint partner but not so late that he couldn't get up early and pick up his mom. He would do anything for her.

"All right then, it's settled. I'll go see my doctor tomorrow." She gave Terry a smile. "Now can we have a normal meal? Without everyone getting all upset about stuff?"

It took a little while for the conversation to get going, but after a while, it felt pretty normal. Roland figured that everyone was trying to come to grips with it as he had been for a while now, and he was ahead of the curve. But he appreciated everyone trying to be normal for their mom's sake. She didn't like having the extra attention on her.

The meal was shorter than it normally was, and it was 11:30 when he made it to the tree where he met his partner. He figured he would have a long wait, but she showed up within two minutes of him.

Maybe she was as eager as he was to meet.

Chapter Twenty-Three

"Wow, you're here early. I thought I would beat you by a mile," Nelly said to her Secret Saint partner as he walked up.

"I was a little restless. I had a meal with my family tonight." There was something familiar about his voice, and...it seemed like he didn't have it disguised like he normally did.

"Oh? How did that go?" she asked.

"My mom hasn't been well for a while. At least, I felt like I've seen it and no one else has." The disguise was fully back. Maybe she had imagined it. There was a pause as he seemed to think. "Except for one person. One person that I didn't really expect to be so observant, but they were."

"Oh? Did something happen tonight?" she asked.

She tilted her head, and he leaned back against the tree.

"Yeah. Mom was just—she had slept all afternoon, then when we walked in, instead of helping, she said she'd sit down. And she brought potato chips. She never brings something store-bought to a meal. She always makes something homemade. But it wasn't until she said she would rather sit down than help in the kitchen that my whole family realized there was something wrong."

"Then you were vindicated. Because haven't you said something and they haven't listened?"

"That's right. They haven't. And so yeah, I suppose I haven't told you that my sister is a doctor, and she's going to see Mom tomorrow."

He paused a bit, as though thinking about it, and she thought that maybe he was so wrapped up in what he was thinking that he didn't realize that he had just given away a detail about his family that...she could figure out who he was.

Maybe her brain didn't want to, because it was a little bit slow, but he continued on talking about some of the other symptoms that he'd seen with his mom while Nelly held her breath.

It was Roland. The man speaking to her was Roland McBride.

His sister, Terry McBride, who had married Judd and was no longer McBride, ran the medical center in town. That much was obvious. Of course. He was the exact height, and while he spoke in an affected tone, she could recognize his voice under it.

It was Roland.

She felt shock and felt a little aghast at herself because she...she was pretty sure she was falling in love with him. And that made sense. The fact that as she was working with him on the Christmas play, and as the Secret Saint, and even at the Christmas tree lighting ceremony, she had felt very similar feelings—a calmness and a peace and a security, and she thought again about how their voices blended together. She had felt something touch her soul when their eyes had met, and their voices blended, and they sang together.

She hadn't been able to put her finger on it, but it was the same way she felt when she worked with the Secret Saint.

"Do you think I did the right thing?" Roland finally said, and she realized he'd been talking for a while and now wanted her opinion.

"Of course. You tried to tell your family. They didn't listen. You talked to your mom, asked her to go to the doctor, and she refused.

What were you going to do? Beat everybody over the head and insist that you were right? Kidnap your mom and take her to the doctor? You did what you could."

"I just hope it's nothing serious. She is… She's the anchor of our family. She's been there for us no matter what. She's sacrificed so much for her children, and there's never been any doubt in our minds that we were loved, because of her. Plus, I know she prays for us all every day. It's a blessing to know that you have a mom who cares that much about you. You know?"

"Yeah, and being surrounded by her prayers just gives you a security that I'm sure is a real blessing."

"It really is."

She put a hand on his arm. Normally she didn't touch him.

But this time…she just couldn't keep herself from it. He needed comfort, and sometimes the only comfort that was possible was the comfort of a human touch.

"I think you did the right thing. I know it's hard. Hard to see someone that you know and love and has always been such a rock in your life not be her normal self." Boy, did she know about that, with her gram. And Roland, of all people, had been there to help her.

Now, looking back, knowing what she knew now, she couldn't believe how he had been woven throughout her life but especially throughout this last month. He'd been there for her when she needed someone after her grandma had her episode.

And it kind of explained her fierce response when the pastor had accused him of stealing. She knew he hadn't done what he had been accused of.

"I appreciate that. I guess… I was really looking forward to coming here tonight, just because you're so easy to talk to. Thanks for listening."

"I wish I could do something to help. To make it so that you knew that there was nothing wrong with your mom. Or something along those lines, but I guess I'm just here if you need me."

"That's enough. It's good to know that you have someone you can depend on, you know?"

"Yeah. That's what friends are for." She was definitely friends with Roland. She had felt that the last few times they'd been together, that their antagonism had been buried, and they were actually friends. And she'd always felt that way about her Secret Saint partner. But now... She knew who it was. She debated about whether she should tell him or what to do about it. But what good would it do to let him know that she knew who he was? He might want to know who she was, and...she didn't think she was ready to say. Maybe she never would be. Although, she was kind of curious to know whether he was as drawn to her in their real life as she was to him.

She kind of thought he might be drawn to her as the Secret Saint. He hadn't said so specifically, but he had just said that he really looked forward to talking to her, and they talked about how compatible they were. That didn't really mean a whole lot, but perhaps... She just didn't know. She would keep it to herself for now.

"I hope you don't mind, but I have a friend who's going through a bit of a hard time, and I arranged to have some things dropped off for her. I suppose it's in my Secret Saint capacity, but not really. It was kind of a spur-of-the-moment thing as I was thinking about her, and...she's kind of special to me."

Nelly blinked. That felt like it came out of left field. "No. Of course not. You can do nice things for anyone anytime you want to."

He had someone who was special to him? He was thinking about her?

She felt a pain shoot through her chest and out both arms.

There went that idea. She thought he was falling for her, like she was falling for him. But he had someone else who was special.

"Is there something she needs that the two of us can do together?" she asked, surprised her voice sounded natural. She felt congested inside, like her chest was squeezed tight.

"I'll let you know, thanks." It seemed like he was smiling under his ski mask—it sounded like there was humor in his voice, but she barely registered it.

Now she knew who he was, now she knew that her feelings for him were one and the same—the way she felt about Roland, all rolled into the way she felt about her Secret Saint partner—and now, to find out that he was giving anonymous gifts to a very special person in his life.

Just her luck.

They chatted about what they were going to do the next day, and she had to admit, it was all she could do to try to sound enthused and interested. Because she felt despondent.

They parted thirty minutes later, and Nelly walked slowly to her car.

Figures, she thought as she drove home. *Just figures.*

But she needed to be supportive. He was going through a hard time, and he thought that she was his friend. She wanted to be his friend—actually, she wanted to be more, but even if she couldn't be more, she still owed him her friendship. She needed to support him in whatever way she could.

As she pulled into her regular spot and parked, she noticed that there seemed to be a big box on the front porch.

She got out of her car, walking softly to the porch, looking around a bit to see if there was anything else out of the ordinary.

She walked over and peeked inside. Was someone dropping off Secret Saint supplies?

There was a sheet of paper on top, and she opened it up, tilting it toward the streetlight so she could read it.

"Dear Nelly, I noticed that your grandma seems to be having some difficulties, and I thought you might be able to use these things. Your friend, SS"

She stared at the note, thinking. Could it be true? Roland's special friend, the one that he was deeply affectionate toward, was her.

The butterflies in her stomach started floating around dreamily.

Roland liked her. She wasn't sure how much, but she was definitely special to him. That made her whole heart sing. She dropped to her knees and rooted through the box. It was supplies to help her take care of her gram. There was absorbent underwear, a baby monitor, and a Ring camera, which she wished she would have thought of. She could put it up, and she could check on her gram while she was at school. She could tell her grandma it was there, so it wouldn't be like she was spying on her or anything, but it would give her a peace of mind that she hadn't had in a long time.

She continued to look through the box—more items that would be so helpful, and each new discovery made her smile grow bigger and bigger. And by the end, she was grinning like a fool. Roland was so very, very sweet.

Chapter Twenty-Four

"I don't know my lines," Maryellen said as tears started to fill her eyes.

Roland looked at her. She wasn't going to cry, was she?

He would rather be handling the boys, but Nelly had been working on getting them to stand in the exact arrangement she wanted, and he didn't exactly know what that was. So he was going over lines with the other kids. However, Maryellen, who was playing Mary in the play, looked like she was about to cry, because apparently she didn't know hers.

The wind howled outside as the first real storm of the season blew in.

They had wanted to get practice over quickly so they could hopefully send the kids home, but they needed at least an hour. They'd had fifteen minutes.

"That's not a big deal. We'll just work on them a little. You only have a few, and you're gonna be fine."

"But I'm scared. What if I mess them up?"

"So if your mom was in a play, and she messed up her lines, would that bother you?"

Maryellen looked at him and seemed confused before she slowly shook her head.

"That's what I thought. You're very forgiving. You just want to see your mom up there, enjoying herself and doing a good job, but also having fun. Right?"

"I guess," Maryellen said softly.

"That's what everybody wants for you. There is no one who is going to be angry or upset if you don't remember your lines."

Roland wasn't entirely sure that her family wouldn't be angry if she didn't remember her lines. But her mom seemed like a reasonable person, and he was casual friends with her dad, who was pretty easygoing.

Maybe they were harsh behind closed doors, but...without specific knowledge, he couldn't say. He was just trying to ease her mind.

"I guess you're right," she said, thinking about it.

He was relieved when she apparently decided he was right.

Just then, a particularly fierce gust of wind shook the church building, and the lights flickered.

If the lights went out, it was going to get interesting.

He told Maryellen her lines, and as she repeated them back to him, he lifted his eyes and met Nelly's gaze across the room, where she gently moved a boy about six inches to get him into position before kneeling down and putting a piece of tape on the floor where he should stand.

Her expression said that she too was concerned that they wouldn't get their full practice in, and maybe they should send the kids home.

But that would involve calling all their parents, and by the time they got that done, it would be time for the kids to leave anyway.

He had worked for another five minutes with Maryellen and had pulled Joseph aside to check on his lines when the building shook from the howling wind, and the lights flickered again and then went out.

Some of the children immediately screamed, and others started to cry.

"Hey, guys, hey," he said, waiting until everyone was listening. "It's okay. We're good. If you notice, there's still enough light that we can see each other, because it's not quite dark out yet."

It was getting dark earlier and earlier, but since practice was directly after school, there was still some dusky light coming in through the clouds and the snow.

"I love candles. They're my favorite thing ever. Sometimes when I have a particularly hard day," Nelly said as she moved around, grabbing some things from under the pew before she stood, "I light candles to relax. Don't you guys like candles?"

"Sometimes we eat dinner by candlelight. Mom says it's romantic!" Maryellen said.

That made Roland smile. Only a woman would think candlelight was romantic. Or a bad cook. He supposed it would be harder to see the food if the lights were dim.

His mom had wanted him to date Maryellen's mother. Perhaps that comment hinted that he'd dodged a bullet.

"Exactly. Candlelight is romantic. And it makes a common, ordinary dinner super special."

That was Nelly, and he bit his lip. She thought candlelight was romantic?

She had just said that she enjoyed candles.

And then he realized that what she had grabbed from under the pew was a box of candles, and now she began setting them around and lighting them.

"And candles can make Christmas pageant practice fun and special too," she said cheerfully.

He thought that her words had effectively banished any lingering fear or concern the children had. And now, they watched with smiles as she walked around the sanctuary, setting candles down in strategic spots and lighting them all while explaining about fire safety.

He was impressed that she had been able to turn the atmosphere of the entire room so quickly from fear to eager anticipation.

He walked over, grabbing some candles out of the box and picking up the other lighter. He noted the pattern she was using to set the candles down on the windows along the other side, and he began setting them on the opposite side, lighting them as he went.

"It will probably be dark the day that we do the play, so this is actually really good practice for us. I'm so glad this happened."

"But I don't like the dark," one of the littlest girls said, sounding perilously close to tears.

"I love the dark. It gives you a special, secret place all to yourself for you to snuggle down under your blankets and be completely alone and invisible to anyone else." Nelly smiled. "But we're not completely in the dark, are we? Look how pretty the candles are."

"They are kind of pretty," the girl said tentatively.

Nelly continued to encourage her, and he finished placing the candles around while Nelly stood in front of the children and explained what they were going to be doing next.

He and Nelly had gotten into a rhythm, and it was almost like they could read each other's minds. They worked so well together it was uncanny.

Maybe he had just grown up, since he had the same ability to work with his Secret Saint partner too. He'd never felt anything like it in his life before, and now he had two women that he worked so well with.

His eyes went to Nelly as she was animated and engaged with the children.

She was so good with them. She was born to be a teacher for sure, but there was also a womanly grace about her that pulled him in a way that he wanted to resist.

It was the same way his Secret Saint partner pulled him. Odd that it was happening at the same time in the same way, and he looked back over his life to think about what was different.

His mom for one. Maybe Isadora coming back with her children.

But maybe he was just maturing.

He thought about his sister Terry saying that she had examined their mom and sent her for tests. They wouldn't know the results of the tests for a bit, and she wouldn't be able to diagnose anything in particular until she did.

The waiting was going to be excruciating.

Terry had assured him that she didn't think it was anything serious, but legally she wouldn't have said that to anyone outside the family because she didn't want to get anyone's hopes up and be sued for misstating.

He heard Nelly's voice calling his name, and he came out of his fog of thoughts to join in with the program practice again.

It went better than one could expect for a candlelight practice, and he had to admit he was almost disappointed when it was over. He wasn't sure whether it was the candles, or whether it was just the attitude of the children caused by doing something a little bit different, but the whole practice seemed to take on a fun, Christmasy glow.

Pastor Connelly came in as the last children left. He was a little disappointed because he was hoping to be able to talk to Nelly by herself. He didn't know exactly what he wanted to say… Maybe an apology?

He just knew he didn't want to walk away from her.

"Unfortunately, someone's been stealing money from the donation box again," Pastor Connelly said gravely as the door closed behind the last student, and Nelly stood on one side of the sanctuary, folding up costumes and placing them on the front pew for easy access for the next practice while he walked around and started blowing out and collecting candles.

"Well, then you should know that it's not Roland, at least," Nelly said, and she barely looked up from where she was folding the costumes.

"Actually, again, he's the only one on the video between

yesterday morning and this afternoon when I counted the money just before the children arrived."

Nelly looked stricken, and Roland almost smiled. After all, she had so much belief in him that the idea that he would be on the camera again was absolutely shocking to her, obviously.

"I had to come in. I brought the box of costumes in from the storage shed where we keep them. I said I would do that, and I did."

"And you helped yourself to another hundred dollars while you were at it," Pastor Connelly said.

"No. I didn't," Roland said, keeping his voice calm. It made him a little bit angry that the pastor immediately jumped to that conclusion, but he understood why the pastor might. It was hard— he was on the video both times the money had been stolen, but he also knew for a fact that it hadn't been him, so there was no point in getting upset. Although it did not feel good, at all, to be falsely accused.

"Roland had to bring the costumes in. We had asked him to do that, and he did. So obviously of course he was going to be on the video."

"But there was no one else there. I went through the entire thing."

"Well, then something else is going on, because Roland said he didn't do it, and we all know that he's not a thief."

It surprised him that she was still defending him, even with what amounted to more "evidence" against him.

"Do you have the camera pointing at the actual container?" Nelly asked, as though she had just considered that he was only accusing Roland of coming in, not saying that he actually saw him take it.

"No. I really should get a camera that is pointed there. When we had our security system installed, it was installed to police the front of the building. We don't have cameras in the back, and we don't have cameras inside."

"Well, why don't you get an inexpensive camera just for this purpose and put it there for this week?"

Pastor Connelly flattened his lips. "I'm going to go to the police with this. I just wanted you guys to know. But your idea of a camera is a good one, and I'll have to take it before the board, since I can't really do anything by myself."

Nelly didn't say anything, but her lips pressed down, and he knew she wasn't happy. It was really sweet of her to be so passionate in defending him. It confused him a bit, though, considering that the two of them had never been great friends. Sure, he thought they were getting along pretty well now, but...after their history, he would have thought that Nelly would have at least been suspicious.

Pastor Connelly left and went down the hall to his office, closing the door behind him.

He finished blowing out the candles on his side, carefully carrying them so the wax didn't drip on the floor as he walked around the back and started up the other side. He met Nelly halfway down as they blew out the last candle together. It was rather dark in the church after that, but he held the last three candles in his hands while the wax firmed up and pulled his phone out with his other hand, turning the flashlight on.

"That was a great idea about the candles."

She laughed. "The kids loved it too. And I don't know that it was ever my dream exactly to have the Christmas program practice by candlelight, but I've always loved candles, and there's just something about lighting a candle that somehow makes the room feel more cozy."

"I've never noticed, but...it was a fun practice."

"Yeah, it really made a difference in the whole atmosphere. Funny how just something little can do that."

"Yeah." He was quiet for a moment, and she kind of stood there. Whether she was waiting for him to say something, or whether she had something of her own to say, he wasn't sure. But he was kind of scrambling for words. Finally, he said, "I just wanted to thank you."

"For the Christmas program practice? If I wasn't doing it, somebody else would."

"No. For defending me. I... I know that we haven't exactly been friends over the years, and it surprises me that you are so adamant about my character."

"I know we didn't get along for a really long time, and as I look back, I can see that it was because of my misconceptions. My hurt colored how I felt, and I never allowed myself to get over it. But if I'm being honest, you're really a nice person. I was the one who refused to see." She lifted her shoulder and shook her head. "You have impeccable character. You've never been dishonest or stolen anything, and everyone who knows you believes the best about you. I'm not sure I understand why Pastor Connelly is so down on you."

"I think he just feels like he has the evidence in front of him and there's no other conclusion to come to, you know?"

"I thought of that. Also, he's probably really upset that someone would dare take money from the church, and he just wants it solved, you know?"

"Doesn't want to dig too hard, because where else can he dig?"

"Exactly."

"Anyway, thanks. I appreciate it."

Nelly nodded her head. "Anytime."

As they walked out, Roland thought of something that he could do for Nelly—it was just a little thing, to kind of say thank you for the way she was defending him. He was determined to do it soon.

Chapter Twenty-Five

Supper was over, and her grandma sat napping on the couch.

Usually Nelly took a little nap herself, to get ready for meeting her Secret Saint partner, or she might correct papers in her chair, although she didn't have anything to do today. She'd been going pretty light on the kids since Christmas was so close.

She felt torn though. She was definitely attracted to her Secret Saint partner. He was generous and kind and thoughtful and very much loved the Lord, and he was concerned about bringing glory to God and not about making himself look good.

And then the more time she spent with Roland McBride, the more she felt a definite attraction to him as well. And now that she knew the Secret Saint *was* Roland...the feelings had multiplied. She had no idea how he felt about her, but...the confusion and uncertainty in her own heart was real.

She pulled out her phone and dialed the number of the one person who had always given her fabulous advice, her old college roommate, Kate Woolbert.

She hadn't talked to Kate for a month at least, since both of them were teachers, and this time of year was crazy busy for any teacher.

Kate was probably working on programs at her school, if not at her church as well, and there were always extra activities in the classroom this time of year.

It wouldn't have shocked her if Kate hadn't answered, but the phone only rang three times before she heard her friend's voice.

"Nelly! It's so good for you to call me!"

"It's nice to hear your voice. It's been a long time."

"I know. Considering that when we first started teaching, we were talking every day."

"Twice a day, morning and evening. I think we needed the moral support. It's not for the faint of heart."

"No. I was scared to death I was gonna ruin an entire classroom full of kids when I first started."

"Me too. And it was nice to know that I wasn't the only person in the world who felt like that."

They had had many shared conversations that first year especially, and then as they slowly became almost veteran teachers, their conversations became more about their lives and less about their students, although they still enjoyed exchanging stories.

"What's going on?" Kate asked, and Nelly gave her a few updates on her life and then asked about hers.

After they were done getting each other up to speed on the various things that were going on, Nelly finally waited for a break in the conversation, and then she said, "I've got a little bit of a problem, and I wanted your perspective on it."

"It's about a man, isn't it?" Kate said immediately, laughing.

"How'd you guess?" she said with a chuckle.

"Woman's intuition, right?"

They shared another moment of laughter, and then Nelly said, "So I told you that I'm doing some Secret Saint work."

"Right, and that's just basically like a Secret Santa, only townwide."

"Yes. And no one knows my identity. What I didn't mention is that I have a partner."

"Oh? Tall, dark, and handsome?"

"I'm not sure. He is tall, taller than me anyway, but I have no idea what he looks like."

"Intriguing."

"Right?" Nelly took in a deep breath and blew it out, trying to figure out where to start. "Anyway, we work well together, and…I've already found out that he's about my age and he's not married."

"Those are important details to know."

"Right, and then he was telling me about some issues that he had, and…when he gave me the details of his family, I was able to piece a few things together and figure out who he was."

"Okay."

"Do you remember the guy I told you about that I was always in competition with in high school and elementary school?"

"The one who got the valentine that you accidentally gave to the wrong person, and he made fun of you?"

"Yeah. That one."

"Oh my goodness, he's the Secret Saint that you've been working with?"

"Yes. We're doing the Christmas program together too. Through our own volunteering, we kind of got pushed into it. So it's not like he's secretly trying to be with me."

"Okay. And does he know your identity as a Secret Saint?"

"No. He doesn't, at least—I've been very careful to try to make sure that he doesn't. So unless he recognizes my voice, he hasn't seen me or anything of me, except my hands."

"Okay. Are you wearing jewelry?"

"No."

"All right."

"So… I don't know whether to tell him that I know who he is or not. And this feeling that I have, this… I work better with him than I've ever worked with anyone, and I just feel—I don't know, protective of him somehow, and attracted to him for sure, but I don't know how he feels about me. And I don't know what to do about it. Should I tell him I know who he is? Should I tell him that I'm attracted to him? I mean, that's gonna be really embarrassing if he only likes me as a friend."

"Right, so that's the con, but the pro of that is that he might like you for more, so you have a lot to gain if he does."

"And you're saying that that is better than the potential embarrassment if he doesn't."

"Right."

"Or should I tell him that I'm his Secret Saint partner first?"

"Yeah. I would definitely do that, and I would do it as soon as possible."

"Why? I keep telling myself that it's better to keep our identities a secret."

"It is, if neither one of you knows who the other is, but if you know something that he doesn't, you're hiding it from him and not the rest of the town. And...how would you feel if he knew who you were, and he didn't tell you?"

Nelly sat and thought about that for a while. It was always good to try to put herself in someone else's position and try to figure out how she would feel about it.

It didn't take her long to figure out that she would want to know. And she would feel betrayed if Roland actually did have feelings for her, knew who she was, and didn't tell her. After all, wasn't that the bedrock of any relationship—that you were honest and open with each other?

"I would want to know," she said simply.

"That's what I thought."

"So I need to tell him who I am, and then you think I need to admit that I'm attracted to him?"

"Now that, I don't necessarily think you need to admit immediately. I mean, you'll get hints from him about whether he kind of feels the same. Like, there's no need to put yourself out there unless you have an inkling that you're not going to be embarrassed. You can kind of get an idea that you're not going to, first."

"Right." She let out a breath. "Thanks for clarifying that for me. I don't know why I struggled with it so much. To say or not to say, how long to keep the secret, all of that. You know?"

"Yeah. You know, the other thing that you could do is just ask him. If you guys talk as easily as you say you do, just say, 'Hey, if I figure out who you are, do you want me to tell you that I know?'"

"Then he'll pretty much know that I know."

"Exactly. And then he'll know whether he wants to know, and then he'll be able to tell you whether he wants to know who you are. Make sense?"

"Yeah. Good point." It was always good to just talk about things rather than make assumptions or act on partial information, when she could get everything she needed.

"So I was thinking about coming back home," Kate said after they'd been silent for a bit and Nelly had been thinking about hanging up.

"For a visit?" Nelly said, immediately excited that her friend would be coming home.

"No... For good."

"But you just said you were really happy there. You were involved in so many things! It's all going really well, I thought."

"Well, I'm making it work, but...I thought working in an inner-city school would be rewarding, and it is when I work with the students, but there are so many things they want me to teach that I don't believe in, and the culture and attitude here is just... It's so much different than our beautiful small town, you know?"

"You're homesick," Nelly said simply.

"Yeah. I'm definitely homesick."

But it was more too. Nelly could tell from the tone of her voice that she was deeply unhappy with the direction things were going at the school district she worked at.

"Whoever's in charge usually makes a big difference in the general atmosphere of the school."

They were blessed enough in Mistletoe Meadows to have a really amazing school counselor, but...she thought that person might be leaving.

"You know what, you've been working on getting your credentials—do you have them?"

"I should finish up at the end of this year, if I can stand four more months of working and going to school as well. I'm tired."

"It's a lot. But the school counselor position might be opening up here in Mistletoe Meadows. I can keep an ear to the ground for you."

"That's awesome. Now that I know that, I can keep an eye out for it myself too. But do please let me know if you hear anything."

"I absolutely will. I would love it if you came back in that position. That would be wonderful."

"Wouldn't it?" Kate said with a sigh.

"All right. I've kept you long enough." She saw her grandmother stir and figured she probably ought to try to get her to bed and then take a little rest herself.

"Thanks for calling," Kate said.

They hung up shortly afterward, and Nelly sat there for a moment, feeling so much better after having talked to someone. Of course, she needed to let Roland know she knew who he was. And then he could decide whether he wanted to know who she was. Maybe she should do that tonight.

Chapter Twenty-Six

*R*oland checked his watch—he was going to be really early.

He'd managed to get the box to Nelly's porch, and he smiled at the thought of her opening it.

She might even guess that it was from him. But hopefully it wouldn't allow her to figure out his identity as a Secret Saint.

But if she did... He was really hoping they could develop something more in their relationship, and having her guess who he was wouldn't be the worst thing that ever happened.

In fact, he wondered if maybe subconsciously he was hoping she would.

Regardless, he slipped back into his pickup and drove to the tree.

He was pretty sure he saw his partner Secret Saint's cloak moving gently in the wind in the shadows as he arrived at twenty after eleven.

The entire town was deserted though, so it wasn't a big deal. He did think it was funny that both of them seemed to be getting there earlier and earlier. He didn't know why she was, but he was eager to see her and could hardly wait, and couldn't keep himself from leaving his house way before he needed to.

They needed to talk about some of their Secret Saint activities, and he figured he would give her an update on his mom, letting her know that she was going for test results. It was nice to know that someone was praying for her. And... He thought about Nelly. She would pray for him too.

He felt torn between the two of them. Funny that they both seemed so similar, but he knew they weren't the same. He was absolutely sure of it.

It had to have been him and some change he'd made in his life that all of a sudden had him getting along and working well with others.

He couldn't just fall in love with every person he ever worked with. That would be a rather debilitating issue to contend with.

"Hey there," he said as he stopped beside the tree. He wasn't sure why she hadn't moved out of the shadows of the other tree that wasn't very far from the one they met at. Sometimes they would wait at that one, since it was a little bit more sheltered.

"Good evening," she said, and her voice sounded a little different. Familiar, but before he could figure that out, she stepped out of the shadows and walked forward.

She wore her cape, but the hood was down.

He noticed that right away. And his heart stopped beating. He turned away immediately.

"You forgot to put your hood up," he said. Still, something nagged at him. Her voice. He knew it.

And the glimpse that he'd had of her hair and face.

"No. I didn't forget. I left it down on purpose. I have a confession to make."

"But we said we weren't going to let each other know what our identities were." Why was he panicking? That should be a good thing. He was just thinking he wanted to know who she was, wanted to know the name of the woman he seemed to be falling in love with.

"That's my confession. I didn't want to, didn't mean to, but when you were talking about your mother, I figured out who you were."

Of course. He had said his sister was a doctor. He wanted to slap his forehead, but instead, he turned slowly around.

He had just recognized the voice.

It was Nelly.

And yes, his eyes confirmed what his brain had just figured out. Nelly Bushnell stood in front of him, wearing the Secret Saint cape that had become familiar and beloved to him, only the hood was down, and her hair reflected a muted version of the moonlight above.

"Nelly," he said, felt her name curl off his tongue, and it all made sense now. He wasn't falling in love with two different people. He wasn't unable to keep from falling in love with every person that he worked with. It was the same person. No wonder he felt torn. No wonder he felt drawn to both of them.

"You," he said, when she said nothing, waiting, probably to see his reaction. She'd already figured it out and had her reaction.

"What do you think of working with me? Was it a surprise?" he finally asked, wishing that she had explained to him how she felt, how it had changed things between them, if it had at all.

"I was really, really surprised. And I resisted at first, because we had agreed that we weren't even going to try, and I wanted to honor that, but there was just no way I couldn't keep my brain from making that connection once you talked about your sister being a doctor. I mean, the only doctor in town is Dr. Terry."

"I know. An amateur mistake, I guess," he said, a little bit of humor entering his tone. He was adjusting to this idea.

"I wasn't terribly upset about it. In fact, I had started to develop a different opinion of you from working with you with the children's program, and after that, and—"

"That's why you defended me."

"No. I didn't know you were the Secret Saint when I first started defending you. I just... I've known you from before we even went to school. I knew that wasn't something you would ever, ever, ever do. Pastor Connelly is wrong about that."

"Yeah. He is."

"And then, when I did realize your identity, I knew that you weren't going to be altruistic by night and steal money from the church by day. It didn't even make any sense. But of course, I couldn't say that to the pastor."

"No. You couldn't." Wow, it had been Nelly all along. And she had defended him before she even knew he was a Secret Saint. That made his heart swell, and he almost put his hand over his chest because the feeling was so odd.

"I haven't known for very long. I honestly wasn't sure what to do with the information. We had decided that we weren't going to try to figure each other out, but we hadn't decided what we were going to do if one of us did figure it out. And I finally decided that if it were me —if you knew, and I didn't—I would want you to tell me. So the only thing I could do once I figured that out was to tell you. You know?"

"Wow. That makes a lot of sense, and I appreciate your honesty. Not everyone is like that."

"It's the way I wanted to be treated. And...I felt like it was fair. You know?"

She seemed like she was a little uncertain, and he wanted to ease her mind. After all, it had taken a certain amount of bravery in order for her to put her hood down and walk toward him.

"Nelly." He laughed, huffing out a breath that was half laugh, half amazement, shaking his head at his own stupidity. "I should have figured it out. Of course. It all makes sense now."

"You're not upset? I know I'm not your favorite person." She sighed. "You've been kind to me at church, but I figured that might just be because of the children and working with them. After all, you can't just do what you want when there are other people involved. And you've been very mature about it."

"Well, you're right. We had to get along, we couldn't indulge the way we felt with no thought to how that would affect everyone else.

You know, sucking it up for the greater good." She laughed a little, and it made him smile. "I like it when you laugh."

She didn't say anything, but he could almost see her brows going up and her eyes widening.

He swallowed, realizing his throat was rather dry and he was all of a sudden nervous.

"Is this going to change anything?" he asked. He really wanted it to, but at the same time, he only wanted the changes to bring them closer together. He didn't want things to change so that she decided to quit being a Secret Saint or distance herself from him.

"It doesn't have to." She paused and then said, almost as though she were afraid of his answer, "Unless you want it to."

"No!" he said almost too quickly. And it wasn't quite true, but he didn't know how to explain why it wasn't. Because he did want it to change. He wanted... He wanted her to love him the way he loved her, but a person couldn't control that. They couldn't make someone else feel something that they didn't.

But he couldn't quite get up the nerve to ask her if she might ever be able to feel for him the way he felt for her.

Maybe he could just give it a little bit of time and see if she responded to him and any overtures that he might make.

"Unless you do?" he added, knowing that he sounded as uncertain as he felt.

"No!" she said softly yet fiercely. "I don't. I love the work that we've been doing. I love helping people, and the feeling that gives, and the way I know that I am being the heart and hands of Jesus." She paused for a moment, and then she said, "And I love working with you."

"Well, then it's settled," he said, relief making his chest feel light. "Nothing has to change."

"No. Nothing has to change."

Her words hung in the air between them, and he didn't realize it, until he had moved closer, close enough to see her eyes wide and looking up into his, feel her breath on his face, and move his hand to touch her hair, moving it back. When she didn't move away from that, he allowed his fingers to trail down, his thumb to touch the lobe of her ear while his fingers touched her neck.

"I didn't realize it was you hiding behind that cloak all the time," he said, and then realizing that he no longer needed it, he reached his hand up and pulled his ski mask off. "I guess I don't need to hide anymore, since you already know who I am."

"No. But we still need our disguises if we're going to be anywhere where we might get caught on camera."

That caused a sour note to enter into his happiness. "Like the church."

"It's the outside that has a camera."

"Yeah."

"I know that's not you," she said, and there was no question in her voice.

"You know how nice it is to have someone who believes in you?"

She smiled. "I think that's my job as a teacher, to believe in my kids, but it's different with you."

"Your kids are lucky." He didn't really mean lucky. He meant blessed. Her kids were blessed to have her behind them, but then he realized that he was just as blessed, because...she believed in him too.

Maybe that idea didn't make him as happy as it should have, because he was in the same category as her third-grade class was, and that wasn't where he wanted to be.

"I guess I'm blessed too," he said, and he heard the flat tone that had entered his voice, almost as though he were disappointed about it.

"You're a little different than my third-grade class," she said, as though she were reading his mind.

His brows went up, and then he figured he could take that one of two ways. Either it was obvious that he was different, because he was a man, or she was saying that he was special.

"Different in a good way? Special?" he asked, wondering if she would catch the difference.

"You're definitely special," she said.

He stood there, processing. And then the thought occurred to him that he didn't have to figure this out this second. He could let it unfold naturally. He didn't have to push. It was enough that they now knew each other's identities, and they could get used to that.

He dropped his hand from her hair and noted that she hadn't moved away from him.

"I'm going to enjoy working with you, Nelly."

"I already enjoy working with you, Roland," she repeated.

And then, because he figured it needed to be said, he began, "I'm sorry for my part in our childhood feud. I was not very kind to you with that valentine, and...I think part of it was because I was jealous."

"Jealous?"

"Yeah. I had a sizable crush on you, and that was a really nice valentine, and at first, I was excited because you had given it to me, but then I saw that it wasn't really meant for me."

"Oh," she said, her eyes widening as comprehension dawned.

"Yeah. That was not what I wanted to see from you, and then to know that you had a crush on someone else, when I thought you were the cutest thing in the classroom, I guess... I lashed out, and I was not kind."

"And I reacted terribly. It never even occurred to me that you might have been doing that because you were jealous."

"That's funny, because of course you wouldn't, but yeah."

"You'd think I'd know. I teach third graders every single day and have for years. I should have figured that out before now."

"Don't worry about it. I guess I was just a really good actor."

"And I was a sore loser."

"You were hurt, and you were lashing out."

"But I didn't have to carry it on for two decades."

"That's a good point. But I helped you. I competed as well."

"You weren't nearly as into it as I was."

"Maybe not, because... I think I always secretly wanted the best for you, you know? I guess I never really got over the crush I had on you." He shook his head. "Not that I would ever have admitted that to myself."

"This means we're burying the hatchet once and for all?"

"Absolutely. I wish we'd done it years ago. I enjoy working with you. And I think we work well together."

"Same."

They stared at each other for a bit before he moved away, and they began to talk about the different things that they had planned for the next night's Secret Saint activities.

There might have been a part of him that was worried that once he found out who he was actually working with, the Secret Saint excitement would diminish. But if he were being honest, finding out that it was Nelly only made him want to do it more.

It was definitely some of the best news he'd had in a long time.

Chapter Twenty-Seven

The following morning, Roland strolled into his mother's kitchen, whistling a happy tune that would make Mr. Rogers and his whole neighborhood proud, despite the fact that his current mission was to take his mother to her doctor's appointment to find out the results of her tests.

Still, Roland couldn't keep the smile from tugging his lips up as he thought about the evening before. Nelly was his Secret Saint partner. And he actually liked her.

He might even be falling for her.

He had trouble thinking of anything except how much he wanted to see her again, which would be at the Christmas program practice tonight.

"Someone sounds happy this morning," his mother said as she set her empty coffee cup down on the bar and pushed her stool away from the counter.

"I suppose I am. But it's the Christmas season. Isn't everyone happy?" It was a rhetorical question, because his mother could easily shake her head no. Not only was she probably nervous about her test results, but his sister, Isadora, was facing the second Christmas with her husband gone. The first one with her divorce finalized.

That couldn't be a happy time.

Still, while Roland felt for both his mother and his sister, he also didn't feel like muting his own happiness would make their sadness or anxiety any better.

His mother gave him an interested glance, and Roland met her gaze.

"I think you have news," his mother said, and... He and Nelly hadn't said that they weren't going to tell anyone. And maybe it would take his mom's mind off of whatever was going to happen at the doctor's office.

So he grinned and nodded. "You'll never guess who I'm now friends with."

"Nelly Bushnell," his mother said.

His brows drew down immediately. "How did you guess?"

"Mother's intuition." His mother gave a knowing chuckle, which coming from anyone else might have grated on Roland's nerves, but instead, it made him smile.

"Really?" He wondered what else her intuition told her. Perhaps she already knew, had maybe even known before he did, that he was falling in love with her?

"So what brought this on?" his mother said with another chuckle and a gleam in her eye.

He opened his mouth, but his mom put her hand up.

"You're going to thank me for volunteering you to help with the Christmas program, aren't you?"

Roland had wondered what he was going to say. He could hardly tell his mother that they had both been the Secret Saint this holiday season.

He hadn't even thought about using the Christmas program as an excuse, but it didn't feel like lying. After all, it was Nelly defending him that had kind of turned his mind toward her, even before he knew that she was the Secret Saint.

"I suppose I owe you for that, along with a million other things that you've done for me since I was born."

His mother waved a hand and grabbed her purse from where it sat on the counter. "You don't owe me anything. You've turned into such an amazing young man, I couldn't be more pleased. Seeing you walk with the Lord and serve Him is all I could ever want or need."

She seemed sincere about that too, and he believed she probably was. Not only did his mother not typically go around talking about or saying things that she didn't mean, but all through his childhood she had always emphasized that that was the end goal: to bring glory to God. Not just for her children, but for herself. And to see a child that she had raised striving to do the same thing probably truly did make her happy.

"Are you ready to go?" his mother asked as she moved toward the door.

Maybe he'd been a little wrapped up in his own thoughts and feelings, the glow from last night, and knowing that Nelly and he had a friendship that he hoped might turn into more, and that he might be falling head over heels for a really wonderful, amazing woman.

But he hadn't noticed that his mom seemed... totally at ease and completely at peace.

"Aren't you nervous?" he asked as he strode toward the door, opening it for his mom so she could step out into the chilly morning air.

"Not in the slightest," she said simply.

"Because you believe that the test results are going to come back normal?" He felt like she was probably lying to herself if she had told herself that. Something was causing her exhaustion, and it could be something extremely serious. Something life-threatening.

He tried to shove that thought aside. He didn't want to think about losing his mother. She had been the rock all through his life, and the idea that she might not be at the head of their family, gently guiding each of them to walk with the Lord, there with her words of wisdom, her calm strength, her beautiful example that he could look at anytime he needed to—the idea that she wouldn't be there... He could hardly stand it.

"No. I understand that I might get very bad news. I'm hoping I don't, but the possibility is certainly there."

"But you seem so... calm. Like you have total peace."

They'd made it to the car, and he opened the door for her and she started to sit before she said.

"I do. Whatever God wills is right. This is obviously something I can do nothing about, so God is in control of it. For me to think that I could do better by worrying or getting upset—it's silly."

She closed the door and he walked around his pickup, trying to figure out what to say.

Finally, as he opened the door, he could do nothing but blurt out, "But you might die!"

His mother just smiled. A peaceful, serene smile.

"I know. And then I would see Jesus. My parents are in heaven, and I have a baby that I lost in a miscarriage. She's there too. I can't wait to see her. There are lots of friends and family, your dad. So many people that I can't wait to be reunited with. Dying is part of life. And... I don't want to die. I want to stay here and be with my kids, to see them grow up. Nothing brings me greater joy than to see my children walking in truth, but if God wants me in heaven, I'm ready to go."

He jutted his chin out and gritted his teeth. He didn't want to hear that. He wanted his mother to be saying that if they got bad news, she was going to fight it, she was prepared to do whatever possible to live as long as she could. He didn't want to hear her say she was ready to go.

But, even as he marshaled the arguments in his mind, he knew his mother was right. Her thoughts were exactly in line with what they should be. And that's how he should feel too. Except he didn't.

"Did I upset you?" his mother finally asked after he had been quiet for the first few minutes of the ride.

"Is it that obvious?" he said with half a breath. He wasn't mad, he was just... he loved his mom, and he didn't want anything to happen to her.

He tightened his grip on the steering wheel. "I know you're thinking the right way. To let God handle it, and that whatever He does is right, but I don't want to let God handle it, because what if God doesn't do what I want Him to?" There. That was the problem. And that was almost blasphemy to admit, because how could The One who had created not just him, but the entire universe, be wrong? He couldn't. And yet... he couldn't trust Him with his mother.

"I know that's the wrong attitude, and I know you have the right attitude. I just... I don't want anything to happen to you."

He couldn't look at her while he was talking, and was grateful for the fact that he was driving and didn't have to take his gaze off the road.

"I think that's perfectly normal, and I wouldn't feel bad about it. I don't necessarily think that God is surprised by that attitude. After all, He knows everything."

His mother gave a gentle smile, and the irony was not lost on him. He wasn't supposed to be upset. He knew that God would not be surprised at his attitude, because God knew everything, and that wasn't hard to accept. But somehow, when he tried to tell himself that God knew everything, and meant that He knew what would be best for him and his mom, whether the test results were positive or negative, it was a little bit harder to handle.

"Yeah. Sometimes, even though I think of myself as a really logical person, logic is not working on me right now."

"I don't think that faith is logical. Faith is actually allowing things that do not seem logical to be okay."

His mom always had such wisdom.

"See? I need you. I need you to share your wisdom with me, because I'm not ready to do life without it." Even though he was old enough and most people would think he was crazy. But... why would he go through life without his mother's wisdom, when he could go through it with it, and do a much better job of living the way he wanted to, in a way that he wouldn't regret?

He pulled into the medical center, a Christmas carol softly playing on the radio, the green wreath Terry had on the door of her clinic proclaiming the season, although the conversation with his mom made him feel less like Christmas than he had in a long time.

And he had been so happy. Why not stay happy? Why not just trust that God knew what was best? Simply trust. Wasn't that what the old hymn said? That to trust and obey was the way to be happy in Jesus?

It sounded so simple, and yet sometimes it was so hard to do.

Still, he didn't want the shadow of gloom and doom hanging over him when his mother seemed so peaceful and serene.

What was the point in being a Christian, if he chose to worry and fret rather than simply trust?

"I'm sorry that I wiped the smile off your face," his mother said, the line between her brows showing her concern as she laid her hand on his forearm, which had not moved from the steering wheel.

"No. It's not your fault, it's mine. You have the right attitude. God knows best, and I just need to leave this in His hands, and choose to be content. Isn't that what Paul said?"

His mother nodded, and he listened as the words to the verse rolled off her tongue, her voice so familiar and beloved, as she quoted the words that were etched in his heart. "I have learned in whatsoever state I am, therewith to be content."

The days of him being able to hear his mother quote Bible verses were numbered.

Of course they were. They'd been numbered since he had been born, but only God knew the number, and what God did was perfect and right. He believed that to the bottom of his soul, and now, this was the kind of challenge that he had in order to prove that what he believed was actually the way he lived. Because if he believed that God was in control, and that He worked everything out for his good and God's glory, then there was nothing to worry about.

"All right, let's go see what the doctor has to say," he said, as he gave his mother a smile.

She looked deeply into his eyes for a moment, as though trying to judge whether he was just putting on a facade, or whether it was sincere to the depths of his soul.

She seemed satisfied with what she saw, because then she returned his smile.

"Let's go."

Chapter Twenty-Eight

"It's cancer," Terry said after she stepped into the room, clutching the clipboard to her chest, her eyes going from her mother to Roland again.

Marjorie sat on the examination table, with Roland standing beside her.

Roland wished he would have taken a seat, because his knees felt weak. He had just determined that he was not going to fret or worry, but the C-word had a tendency to knock the legs out from under anyone.

"What's the good news then?" Marjorie asked, her voice sounding serene and elegant, as always.

Terry looked harried, because the waiting room had been full of people, and she had more work to do than she could keep up with. She shook her head.

"Leukemia. It's a treatable kind, but I want more tests to confirm before I lay out a treatment plan. I've already been in contact with some of the best doctors in the country on this, and I'm determined that we will spare no expense—"

Marjorie put a hand up. "Do I get a say in this?"

"Of course, but you want to have the best chances of surviving this, right?"

All of a sudden Roland's throat closed up tight, and his whole body felt like it was contracting in on itself. He wanted to curl up in a ball, because he could almost guess what his mother's next words were going to be.

"Maybe I don't want to fight this. Maybe I just want to let things take their natural course."

"But Mom, leukemia is usually very treatable."

"I understand. I'm not saying that I don't want to treat it. I'm just saying... I'd like to think about it."

Terry's eyes got big, and then she looked at Roland, as though expecting him to throw in on her side.

He shrugged his shoulders. "I'm here to support her. I... I don't necessarily agree, but Mom is closer to God than I am, and she trusts Him. I wish I had her faith."

"You're developing your own, son," his mom said, patting his hand and giving him a benevolent smile, almost as though he'd done something she was proud of.

"Mom, you know that medicine is not anti-Bible, right?" Terry asked, almost as though she were panicking, scared that her mom was somehow anti-medicine or something.

"My daughter is a doctor. Of course, I think that modern medicine is perfectly okay to practice, and I have nothing against most things that doctors do." Their mom didn't mention anything that she might disagree with, but Roland didn't have too much trouble thinking of some medical procedures that perhaps weren't in line with what the Bible taught.

"But, I also believe that while God gives us medicine so we can use it to help heal our bodies, I also believe that it's not necessarily the first thing we should try, and I'm not necessarily talking about healing myself. I'm talking about allowing nature to take its course."

"So you're not talking about alternative medicine. You're talking about dying from leukemia?" Terry asked, and there was an edge to her voice.

Roland felt bad for her. All of her training must be rebelling at this conversation, and it was with her own mother. So her emotions were involved as well. This might well be the hardest conversation Terry had ever had in her life.

"Yes. If that's God's will. I... I'm not saying that it's wrong to use medicine, or that when someone is sick it's always God's will for them to die. Or if an operation can save someone's life, it's somehow not right to use it. I'm not saying that at all. I'm just saying... Why do we always think that struggling to live is the right choice? Maybe... Maybe sometimes when you get a disease like this, it truly is your time to die."

"But Mom, you're young. You have decades ahead of you. You could live to see your great grandchildren, and possibly your great-great grandchildren. Don't you want to? Don't you think your family needs you? Are you thinking about your children and your family?" Terry seemed to be unable to comprehend why their mother might make a choice like this.

"She has people in heaven who want to see her too, and people she wants to see," Roland added for his mother, although she was perfectly capable of having this conversation on her own. After all, she'd raised Terry to be the wonderful person that she was, the compassionate doctor, the concerned human being. His mom didn't need him to fight her battles for her, but he just couldn't stop himself.

Terry's lips flattened into a line as she folded her arms across her chest, holding the clipboard beside her, and looked between Roland and their mom.

"All right. Of course the choice is yours. I can go over treatment options, and what I think would be best to do, or... We can wait for further tests to come back, and go from there."

"Let's wait for the tests to come back, and in the meantime, let's not ruin anyone's Christmas with this news. The New Year will be plenty soon enough for us to get down to what we need to do in order to either treat this, or to make me comfortable."

The Peace that Passes Understanding seemed to be all over his mother, and she did not look the slightest bit upset or scared.

Terry didn't look nearly so serene, but Roland was pretty sure that would come in time. Terry was a true believer, and her husband, Judd, would probably help her as well.

It wasn't long until they were walking out, and after taking his mother home, eating lunch with her, and then cleaning up while she went back to her bedroom to nap, he spent the rest of the day working at the Christmas tree farm.

And telling himself that everything would be okay. Whether his mother lived, or whether she died, God was in control. And He wasn't going to allow one single thing to happen that wasn't supposed to happen, because he could stop it and change it all if he wanted to.

And in the meantime, it was foolish for Roland to worry or fret.

With that fixed in his thoughts, his mind turned to Nelly, and the fact that he knew his Secret Saint helper. He also thought about the feelings that he had for her, and somehow the idea of his mother's illness made him even more aware of the fragility of life, and the passing of time, and how quickly it went by. He didn't want to waste any more of his life being without Nelly. She made him feel complete in a way that he hadn't felt in a long time. If ever. And he wanted to be with her, forever.

The only problem was, he didn't know how she felt.

Chapter Twenty-Nine

"Thanks so much for coming today," Nelly said to Lilly, smiling at the young girl who did not say anything in return. She hadn't spoken a word since her mother had died three years prior.

"Thanks so much for doing this. She just glows when it's time for me to bring her," her dad, Jack Henderson, put his hand on Lilly's head as he spoke to Nelly.

"It's my pleasure. I couldn't do it without Roland, though," she said, glancing across the sanctuary to where Roland was also greeting parents and giving them updates on how practice went.

She took a few seconds to admire him, before she looked back at Jack, who had added a comment to the effect that Roland's presence had made such a difference and brought so much to the play.

Nelly couldn't disagree. She hadn't wanted to accept any of the ideas that he had brought to begin with, thinking that she did everything pretty well on her own, but a fresh voice, some fresh ideas, and someone who wasn't afraid to get his hands dirty and help out wherever he could, had been invaluable.

Who was she kidding, she thought, as Lilly's hand slipped into her dad's, and they turned and walked away. Roland had made a huge difference, and not just because she knew that he was the Secret Saint, nor because she felt like she was falling in love with him. But because... Working with him was fun. He had challenged her, helped her, and somehow made her better. The way iron sharpened iron.

It wasn't long until the last child walked out, and Nelly found herself tidying up and moving toward Roland.

They had just gotten close enough to chat with each other, when Pastor and Mrs. Tucker came into the sanctuary.

A heavy silence fell on the sanctuary as they waited for the pastor and Mrs. Tucker to walk over to them.

Pastor greeted them, but didn't wait long to say what was obviously on his mind.

"I just wanted to give you an update. Mrs. Tucker and I have added a camera that looks directly at the collection plate. She and I are the only ones who have access to this camera, or who know where it is." He gave a little smile. "Although I did add an 'Under Surveillance' sign out front, since I understand that, even if we do catch the perpetrator, we can't prosecute him using the video unless we have the signs up, warning him that he'll be caught on camera."

"All right," Nelly said, not sure how she felt about prosecuting someone who was so desperate that they felt like they needed to steal from a church.

"I have my eye on you," Mrs. Tucker said, her knowing gaze narrowing at Roland. Then, her lips lifted a little, giving what looked to Nelly like an evil smile, almost as though she was sure that she knew exactly who was stealing, and it was clear that she was implying that Roland was the thief.

To Roland's credit, he let her comments roll off his back.

"I'm glad to hear it. I hope we catch the thief soon. It doesn't sit well with me that the church has been losing donations that have been earmarked for programs like ours. People will stop giving money altogether, if they don't feel like we're going to be using it for good, but instead allow it to be squandered or stolen away."

Roland spoke casually, and if he was upset about Mrs. Tucker's implied and barely veiled accusations, he didn't look like it at all.

The pastor nodded. If he agreed with Mrs. Tucker, Nelly couldn't tell by looking at him. She assumed he was trying to be neutral, but was understandably upset that the money had been stolen.

They talked about how the play was coming for a little bit, and then Mrs. Tucker and the pastor walked away.

"I don't know how you can put up with that. I wanted to rip her throat out," Nelly said as soon as Mrs. Tucker walked out of the sanctuary.

Roland grinned easily, and that grin made the hair on the back of her neck curl and it sent shivers down her spine.

"We'll find out who it is, and then she'll be the one embarrassed for blaming me."

"You're so sure we'll find them. How do you know that they'll steal again?"

"Typically if someone gets away with something, they get braver and bolder. Also," he gave her a mischievous smile, which she couldn't help returning. "I heard that Mrs. Tucker's son, who is a sheriff in a town just south of here, might be moving in with her. Apparently, he's having some trouble with his son, who is an early teen, from what I understood."

"I didn't hear that," Nelly said, lowering her voice and moving closer. Her antagonism toward Mrs. Tucker was almost forgotten in her concern for his son.

Roland nodded. "I'm not sure of the details. Something else might emerge, but I think it has to do with his wife running off with another man, and his son has started acting out. The dad resigned from the police force, and is moving back in with his mother to try to get his son away from the bad influences that he was around in that town. I just thought maybe as Secret Saints we could do something to maybe cheer them up a little, but I'm out of ideas as to what that should be."

"Let me think on it for a little bit. I'm sure we could come up with something. Although, it would be nice if we could have a magic wand to wave over the mom in the situation, to get her to come to her senses, and see how she's destroying her family."

"I could be wrong, but it might be too late even if we did have a magic wand. After someone has cheated, putting a family back together would have to be one of the hardest things that humans can do."

"But with God, all things are possible," Nelly couldn't help but say.

Roland grinned, full on. "I love that positive attitude."

They shared a smile that seemed to stretch between them. As the moment warmed and shimmered, Nelly was tempted to tell Roland how she felt. After all, she felt safe with him. Even if he didn't return her feelings, he wasn't going to make fun of her. But...they had been antagonistic toward each other for so long, maybe they should enjoy this newfound friendship that they had, before she tested it by dropping feelings into the mix. Or maybe she was just too scared to open her mouth. That was probably it more than anything.

They chatted a bit more about a few other things they wanted to do as Secret Saints as Christmas got closer and closer, and then, looking around the sanctuary, and seeing that everything was tidied up, and an entire hour had passed since the children had left, they strolled to the door and reluctantly parted.

Roland watched her leave, excited that they would be together again that evening to deliver gifts to a home. He couldn't wait.

He smiled as she reached her car, then turned around, ostensibly looking for him. She found him, and immediately her face lifted in a smile, as she waved a hand goodbye.

He lifted a hand, not even embarrassed to have been caught watching her, just leaning against the railing of the porch, enjoying the way she moved.

If she thought it odd that he couldn't seem to take his eyes off of her, he couldn't tell.

Thoughts of his mother and worry about her condition threatened to intrude, and he had the most pressing urge to tell Nelly about her. He'd been fighting it throughout the entire evening, because he knew he couldn't tell Nelly when the rest of his siblings didn't know. Still, he knew that Nelly would agree with him that his mother's way was the best, and it would just be nice to be able to talk to someone about it. Funny, until a few weeks ago, he wouldn't have considered that Nelly would be the one person in the world he would want to share the most important news of his life with.

Finally, when her car was out of sight, he pushed off the railing and started toward his own vehicle. Tonight couldn't come soon enough.

Chapter Thirty

$\mathcal{N}$elly pulled her hood a little tighter around her head and quickened her steps. The night air was cool, crisp, and it had the smell of snow in it.

Christmas lights twinkled on the gazebo ahead, and a shadow moved.

Roland.

She smiled to herself.

While Roland knew who she was, and she didn't need her disguise for him any longer, she continued to wear it because neither one of them wanted the entire town knowing who they were. There was something about giving to people in secret that made it more fun. And maybe even more of a blessing, because it definitely couldn't be about them seeking recognition or fame or accolades, if no one knew who they were.

But, there was something really nice about knowing that Roland was her partner. Maybe a few somethings, since her feelings had gotten all jumbled up.

She wanted to talk to him about them so badly, but she didn't want to ruin what they had. It would not just make the Secret Saint projects awkward, but they were working on the Christmas program together too. It had been coming along really, really well.

The shadow moved again, and she caught a glimpse of Roland, his broad shoulders, and even a flash of his smile. He apparently was holding his ski cap.

Her feet moved faster of their own accord, and she found herself a little breathless, as she made it to the gazebo, coming to a stop closer to him than she intended.

"In a rush to get this done before the snow arrives?" he asked, with a smile in his voice.

She nodded. That wasn't exactly what had happened, but it seemed like a good excuse. And, it was true that she didn't want to drive in the snow.

"I have my car parked around the corner. Did you check to see if the house was empty?" That had been their plan. He was coming in from the other direction and they figured that they would meet first, because neither one of them had heard conclusively that the family they were delivering the gifts to was not going to be home.

"I scouted out their house a little bit ago, and saw the car with the parents and kids in it driving away. I assume they're going out like you heard they were going to."

"Perfect. Do you want to come with me? We can drive over together."

She kept her voice low, and managed to keep from reaching out to touch him. Just being near him sent odd tingles of something warm and happy down her backbone.

"Sure," he said easily, and they fell into step together.

He seemed a little quiet as they walked along, and she thought back to the Christmas program, and Pastor and Mrs. Tucker. In particular, Mrs. Tucker and the disapproving frown the woman gave Roland. Was he bothered by that?

"Is everything okay?"

The muted clump of their feet struck the sidewalk four more times before he spoke.

"My mom hasn't been feeling well. I can't really share anything more than that, because she doesn't want my siblings to know. And I can hardly tell someone outside the family when they don't have the information. But... I guess it's weighing on me some."

"This is a terrible time of year to have news like that. And your mom is such a pillar in the community. I'm sure she's just as much the backbone of your family."

"Yeah. I mean, I guess our family won't fall apart if something happens to her, but it feels like it, you know?" He paused for a moment, and then he said, "Plus, I want my kids to know her. I want them to have the blessing of being around her, gleaning from her wisdom, I want that for myself too."

"This sounds pretty serious," Nelly said, thinking that he wasn't talking about any old disease. It sounded like he was talking about something that could kill his mother.

"I guess it has the potential to be." His words were soft. And then a short silence stretched between them. Finally he said, "I feel better just talking to you about it. I'm sorry I brought it up, but I can't share the details."

"No. Don't be sorry. I totally understand. I wouldn't want your siblings to be upset that you shared something with me that they don't even know. And, I get how talking with someone helps. Or even just having someone with you. The day you helped me with my gram really shifted things for me. I... felt like I wasn't alone."

"Anytime you want help, just say so."

"I didn't even have to ask. You just walked in when you heard something was wrong. That... made a difference." That was probably the turning point in her real life, where she started to see Roland as someone other than an antagonist, or her enemy. She started to see him as a man with compassion, and faults, yes, but also a lot of good qualities as well.

"I'm glad I was able to help. Even if it was just a little."

"I feel the same." She was trying to say that it didn't matter to her that he couldn't tell her all the details. She could fill in enough to know that he was talking about something serious, what, exactly, didn't matter. It just mattered that she was there for him.

They had made it to her car, and to her surprise, he followed her to the driver's side, and opened her door for her.

"Thanks," she said, a little flustered as she sat down in her seat. She fumbled with the key before she got it in the ignition while he was walking around.

He had just opened her door for her.

There was definitely a part of her that was swooning inside. How sweet of him. Somehow it didn't shock her that Roland McBride was a gentleman. In fact, she supposed it was what she expected at this point.

"I'm not sure how I got the exact wrong impression of you," she said after he had settled in his seat and they started driving slowly down the street.

"What do you mean?"

"For so many years we were competitors. I thought of you as... Maybe not my enemy, but something close."

"And I was annoyed by you."

She laughed. She couldn't believe that he was just annoyed. She thought more like he probably hated her, but she didn't correct him. "And yet... The way I thought you were isn't the way you actually are."

"I suppose I could say the same," he said.

They glanced over the console at each other, and she had to remind herself to look back at the road.

There was something about him that drew her, something that made her want to tell him that she wanted there to be more between them, but this was probably not the time or the place. Plus, it was like she thought earlier. She didn't want to ruin things between them or make them awkward. And if it turned out that he didn't feel the same, it would definitely be awkward.

How long should she wait?

She was still toying with the question as they got out, and

opened her trunk, pulling out the gifts that she had carefully wrapped over the last week, after she and Roland had gathered them up.

They walked quickly but quietly toward the house, each of them carrying as many gifts as they could.

They made three more trips, until all of the gifts that they had were sitting by the back door, under the porch roof.

"I think that's about it—" Roland started, and then he froze. Headlights flashed, and the low rumble of a car engine came across the chilly night air.

"Quick," he said, his arm coming around her waist, as he pulled her around the corner of the porch, to where a chimney came up against the house, and pressed her into the corner between the house and the chimney.

She had managed to swallow her squeak of surprise as he grabbed her, but now, as he pressed against her, only part of her was listening for the sound of crunching gravel as the car pulled into the unpaved drive.

A car door opened, and then slammed closed, and there were footsteps.

The other part of her felt the warm weight of his body against her, smelled the clean, manly scent, and tried to keep her hands from moving from where they were clenched at her side, to wrapping around Roland's waist, or sliding up his chest and around his neck.

What in the world was she thinking? They could get caught. She should be more concerned about staying still and quiet, and what in the world they would do if someone saw them, than she was in thinking about how good it felt to be pressed against Roland.

The front door opened, and then it closed again, and a light came on, spilling into the yard.

"I only heard one door," Roland said, his voice a soft growl next to her ear.

"Same," she said, thinking back to the car door slamming.

There seemed to be movement in the house as a shadow fell across the light, and then it went out.

Roland hadn't moved, other than his breathing, but she fancied she could feel his heart beating hard against hers.

The front door opened and closed, then footsteps retreated back to the car, and then the door opened and closed again.

Soon the car engine sounded a little louder, and the lights splashed again.

Not long after that, the car disappeared from sight and sound.

"That was close," Roland said, and there was relief in his voice, although he hadn't moved away from her at all.

"Maybe he forgot something."

"That's what I was thinking. Although, at first I thought the entire family was back."

"Yeah."

They didn't say anything for a bit, and still, Roland didn't move. Her head tilted up a bit, and she realized he was staring down at her. As she watched, his throat worked as though he were trying to swallow.

Finally, his voice sounded a little raspy as he said, "Sorry I grabbed you like that."

"You needed to. I hadn't quite figured out what was going on, and if you had tried to talk to me about it, I probably wouldn't have understood at first."

One side of his mouth kicked up a bit, and for some reason, her eyes were drawn to that. She had a feeling that it was his mouth, and the closeness of his body, far more than the near miss of being discovered, that was causing her heart to race and her breathing to be so shallow.

"Nelly," he said quietly, his hand trailing down her cheek.

When had he even raised it? She hadn't noticed. Her hands rested lightly on his waist. When had that happened? She remembered thinking about it, but didn't remember moving at all.

"Roland?" Her voice was soft, a whisper in the wind.

But loud enough to shake him from whatever trance he was in, because his breath hitched, and then he pulled in a deep one before he stepped back.

"I hope I wasn't crushing you," he said, and he seemed to be trying to inject some humor into his tone.

She didn't want humor. She wanted to be kissed. Maybe. Not maybe, for sure. That was what she was hoping would happen. But he seemed... embarrassed, determined to get away from her as soon as possible, if his three steps backward, and the hand adjusting his ski mask was any indication.

"Are you ready to go?" he asked, when she didn't move.

Disappointment spiraled through her. Whatever moment they had, was gone. It was probably for the best. Although, that didn't help her to be any less disappointed.

She was the one who was extra quiet as they walked back to her car, and she drove him to where he had his pickup parked.

They parted amicably, but she felt a little unsettled, even later as she lay in bed.

Was he just unattracted to her? Or was there something wrong with her? Why had he not taken a perfect opportunity to, if not kiss her, at least profess his feelings? Maybe that was because he had no feelings toward her. It was all in her head, what she wished could be, instead of what really was.

And, the fact of the matter was, she had a really, really good friend. Instead of moping around, wishing he could be more, she should appreciate the friendship he had offered, and not constantly wish that it was more. She was going to end up ruining a very good thing.

Chapter Thirty-One

Roland handed Lilly her coat in exchange for her angel uniform.

The little girl smiled at him, and he said, "Great practice, Lilly. You're gonna be awesome tomorrow."

The little girl beamed, as her dad shook his hand.

"I appreciate you doing this along with Miss Nelly. And I really appreciate you finding a role for Lilly where she didn't have to speak, but still felt like she was contributing. It has made her smile more than anything else since she lost her mom."

Jack shook Roland's hand, as Roland nodded.

"It's been fun. I can't deny that it's a lot of work, but to see the kids, and how they've bloomed, has been so rewarding."

He found that he meant every word. It had been rewarding. Of course, he really started looking forward to practice once he and Nelly had started getting along better. And now, he looked forward to every single one. Even if Mrs. Tucker was still giving him suspicious side eyes, and Pastor looked disapprovingly at him every time he walked in the church.

There was nothing he could do about that. No way to prove his innocence. A person was supposed to be innocent until proven guilty beyond a shadow of a doubt. All there were were shadows and doubts, along with unfounded accusations from Mrs. Tucker.

It irritated him, but again, he couldn't let it affect him. Otherwise, he would be angry and bitter and constantly trying to prove his innocence, which would probably only make him look more guilty.

"One more practice in the books," Nelly said as she came over, folding the last angel uniform and setting it down beside where he had set Lilly's on the front pew.

"Now all we have to do is get through the actual performance tomorrow." He smiled down at Nelly. How had he never noticed how beautiful she was?

Maybe she wasn't conventionally beautiful, but her smile was full of life and happiness, and it was liberally given to everyone. She hadn't gotten upset with a single child, and he was the only person that he could ever remember her being angry with.

Last night, he'd almost told her how he felt. Almost. Actually, more than that, he almost showed her how he felt. By kissing her. But that would've been taking unfair advantage of her. After all, she hadn't chosen to be grabbed by the waist and shoved up against the house wall, and even though he was doing it to try to protect both of their identities, he couldn't take advantage of his superior strength, and the situation that had worked exactly to his advantage. He would have felt bad about it.

Probably.

Although, the feeling that he most felt now was regret. Regret that he hadn't taken the opportunity to at least let her know that he thought he was falling for her. To see what she would say. If she could possibly return his feelings.

He didn't believe that feelings were necessary for a good marriage, but it seemed to be the prevailing notion of the day, and he definitely had them for her. But he also knew that she was honest and upright, and would keep her word once it was given. She would stay true to her husband and do her very best to raise her family and her children. Look at how she had taken care of her gram. Look at how she treated the kids in her classroom and even here in the Christmas program. And, she'd never wavered in her support of his innocence, no matter how unkind Mrs. Tucker had been.

"I'm ready," she said, and maybe it was just his imagination, but she seemed out of breath.

He took a step toward her, and started to raise his hand, but was interrupted.

"There's more money missing." The Pastor's voice caused Nelly to startle and take a step back as her head swung around and her eyes widened. The pastor did not look happy.

"Roland, I'm going to have to ask you to show me the money that's in your wallet."

Mrs. Tucker, who was huffing behind Pastor, looked a little surprised at that request.

Roland didn't understand the request either, but he pulled his wallet out of his back pocket.

"I suppose I don't know why you're doing this, but you must have a reason."

"Someone's been messing with the camera. When I try to pull it up on my phone, all I get is static and I can't see anything." The pastor narrowed his eyes. "But I know there's money missing."

"I know there's money missing too, and I know that you have the know-how to figure out how to disable the camera," Mrs. Tucker stopped behind the Pastor, her bosom heaving, her arms crossed over her chest.

Roland had pulled his wallet out of his pocket, and handed it over to Pastor.

But before Pastor could do anything, Nelly said, "Mrs. Tucker, would you be so kind as to let me see your purse?"

"What do you want my purse for?" Mrs. Tucker asked, although at the same time she pulled the strap off her shoulder and handed it to Nelly. Nelly just inspired that kind of confidence in people.

"I'm curious," Nelly said, with a smile.

Then, to Roland's surprise, she gave him a glance, and a look that seemed to say that everything was going to be okay.

Then, Pastor glanced at Nelly, and kind of nodded.

The exchange was odd, but even odder was the fact that Nelly sat down on the pew, and started rooting through Mrs. Tucker's purse.

Pastor sat down beside her, and began to look through Roland's wallet.

Roland had to admit he was baffled, and Mrs. Tucker seemed just as stumped as they stood, almost side-by-side, and watched the odd behavior of Pastor and Nelly.

"Here it is." Nelly's voice did not hold triumph, but instead, it sounded a little subdued, and sad.

In her hand was a twenty dollar bill, and at first Tucker and Roland couldn't see anything odd about it. But then she flipped it over, and he could see a big red smiley face had been drawn on the back.

"I'll be," Pastor said, the few ones and fives that had been in Roland's wallet still held in his fist.

He shook his head. "Mrs. Tucker?" Pastor's voice held so much disbelief and disappointment that Roland almost felt bad for the old lady.

"What? What are you looking at me for? It's not like I'm drawing on money," the old lady huffed.

"No. Nelly came to me with a theory. She convinced me to put a twenty out of my wallet in the collection plate, after I had made a mark on it that would make that bill absolutely unique."

All of a sudden, Roland knew exactly what had happened. And he wanted to kiss Nelly right then even more than he did last night.

"So that you guys would know exactly who the thief was if you caught them with the money in their purse or wallet."

"Purse," Nelly said, looking at him with her eyes shining.

And then, he was sure that she had cooked this up, because she wanted to prove that he was innocent. Although, whether or not she truly thought that Mrs. Tucker had been taking the money, he couldn't be sure. He certainly had never suspected such a thing.

"Mrs. Tucker, I'm sorry, but I'm going to have to go to the police station with this."

Mrs. Tucker's eyes filled with tears, and the starch that held her up proudly seemed to drain completely out of her as her body crumpled into a humble heap. "Please don't. I'm so sorry. You don't understand. After my husband died, the insurance that we got was barely enough to pay for his hospital stay. I couldn't pay for his funeral. I didn't realize that it was going to be so expensive and... I've been struggling ever since! And..."

"I'm sorry. I didn't realize things were so hard for you," Pastor said as he stood and put a hand on her arm.

"I didn't know either," Nelly said, standing up and putting an arm around Mrs. Tucker.

Roland didn't say anything. He hadn't known either, but he wasn't quite sure that Mrs. Tucker liked him. And honestly, he wasn't sure he liked her, since she knew who the thief was all along, and she tried to make it seem like it was him, trying to make him take the blame for her thievery.

But, the old lady was now crying.

"Please don't take me to the police station. I'll pay all the money back. My son is coming to live with me and he's going to pay me rent. With that extra money coming in I should be able to catch up on my bills within a year."

"Or perhaps something else will happen in the meantime," Nelly said, and then she gave Roland a covert glance.

His lips flattened, but he gave a short nod. He knew exactly what she was thinking. As Secret Saints, they had access to a lot of different things, and more than one business had offered to pay off the debts of someone who was struggling. It would be a simple matter of getting that figured out and would take less than a day.

Still, he was irritated because Mrs. Tucker had been so willing to throw him under the bus to protect herself, to use him as a shield for her own sin.

"I owe you a sincere apology. I... I hated the idea that I was soiling your name, but I knew that no one would ever be able to conceivably tie you to the crime. I thought that I would get away with it, and you would be exonerated and everything would work out. I'm sorry. I... I ran your name through the mud and there's no excuse for it."

He'd never seen Mrs. Tucker look so humble. But there was something he didn't understand.

"How did you get in the church without the camera catching you?"

"I have a key to the back door. No one ever thought of that, since I'm the only one aside from Pastor who has one."

"I forgot you even had one."

"I figured."

They all stood there, Mrs. Tucker sniffing, and wiping at her face while Nelly continued to put her arm around her.

Roland supposed it was his turn to talk.

"I accept your apology and forgive you."

There, once the words were out of his mouth, he found that he meant them. He didn't want to hold it against her. He'd certainly done worse things to people, including Nelly. All those years ago he'd insulted and belittled her, because he was jealous of the person she was giving the valentine card to.

"I don't deserve your kindness," Mrs. Tucker said. She hung her head down, and Roland almost hated to see the proud woman looking so humiliated. "My pride wouldn't let me ask for help. I wanted to look competent and like my husband's death was not something that would take any power away from me. When in reality... I could barely function without him. I didn't realize how much I depended on him. I... wasn't expecting to be so lonely, so shaken. I realized I was depending on my husband for my security, rather than God. And then, with the money problems on top of it, I just couldn't admit to the entire church what a terrible Christian I was."

"Everyone is a terrible Christian. No one can live up to the standard that we want to live up to, that Jesus set for us. We're all works in progress," Pastor said, his voice filled with compassion.

"I know that as fact, but I couldn't feel that. I felt like I was the example, and if people knew how terrible I was, I could end up pushing people away from the Lord rather than toward him." She shook her head, irony on her face. "And yet, it never occurred to me that if people found out that I was doing what I was doing, I would be a far worse testimony for Jesus, than showing a little weakness after my husband died, and having money issues."

Roland knew exactly how the old lady felt. There were definitely times where he didn't want to admit his weakness. Even though he still didn't have a whole lot of compassion for her, not like he should, he could totally understand why she did what she did. And he knew, if he were being honest, that he could've done the same thing had he been in that situation. He couldn't imagine being married to someone for fifty or sixty years as Mrs. Tucker had been, and then to try to live life without them. How hard could that be? He had never considered what she might have been going through. He just saw a mean, old lady who was accusing him without any shred of evidence.

"I will make sure to make an announcement in the church tomorrow, during the candlelight program, to let everyone know that you are no longer under suspicion, and apologizing for that to begin with, considering that there was not a shred of evidence for it." Pastor looked back at Mrs. Tucker. "We don't have to tell the entire church what you've done. You can choose to if you'd like to, or you can just keep it to yourself. I... I don't think there's anyone who could judge you for what you did. Anyone could've been in your shoes. As for me, I will not mention your name. I will simply say that we have caught the person who was doing it, they were financially strapped, and had recently lost a close loved one, and have apologized and will be paying the church back. So no charges will be filed."

At that last, Mrs. Tucker's eyes opened wide. "You mean you're not going to make me go to jail?"

Roland couldn't help it. He snorted. Did the lady really think that the pastor was going to have the police arrest one of the upstanding pillars of their community just because she made a mistake? Even he knew that wasn't going to happen.

He glanced at Nelly, and there might have been a small amount of humor in her eyes, but they were mostly filled with compassion and sadness, although when they met his gaze, she gave him a smile of triumph, just to let him know that she was pleased that he was no longer under suspicion.

He stood with the pastor and Mrs. Tucker and Nelly for a bit more, before Pastor and Mrs. Tucker eventually walked away to talk privately in his office leaving Nelly and him alone together.

"Thank you. That was brilliant."

"You don't know how many nights I lay awake, sleepless, because I knew there had to be a way to catch the thief."

"Did you know it was Mrs. Tucker?"

"I suspected. She just... She pushed the idea that it was you so hard, without any evidence, that I thought there almost had to be something between the two of you. Something that you'd done to offend her, or something. But I couldn't figure out anything, even though I asked around town."

"You were asking about me?" he asked, allowing there to be a little bit of suggestiveness in his voice, and just like he hoped, her cheeks pinked.

"You know what I mean. When there wasn't any kind of animosity between the two of you, and anyone I asked always said something along the lines of, the only person that you didn't get along with was me," she rolled her eyes. "After that, I started to think that maybe it really was Mrs. Tucker. After all, why else would she be pushing the guilt on you?"

"That was absolutely brilliant. I never thought of that for one second. But, I can see the logic that you used, and it makes total sense now."

"Well, thank you. I wasn't sure Pastor would go along with it, because he was incredulous when I suggested that it might be Mrs. Tucker, and I was afraid at first that he was going to go straight to her and tattle on me for even suggesting such a thing."

"I'm glad he didn't."

"Me too," she gave him a soft smile, which warmed him to the depths of his soul.

"Are you ready for tomorrow?" she asked, changing the subject and reminding him that he had more to do than just make googly eyes at this woman who he couldn't stop thinking about.

"I think we are. You've done a brilliant job with the kids."

"*We*. We did it together. You and me."

"I kind of feel like I just followed your lead, and tried to be like you, because you have a natural knack with children."

"I'm a school teacher, so I probably have a few tricks up my sleeve, but you do a pretty good job yourself. Do not sell yourself short."

"I won't sell myself short as long as you give yourself the credit you deserve."

They had walked to the door together, and Roland was about to tell Nelly how he felt, even though he had just convinced himself that he shouldn't, when her phone rang.

"I'm sorry, this is my gram. I better answer it," she said, looking up at him with apology in her eyes.

"Go ahead. We can meet tonight. I think I have some sources that will solve all of Mrs. Tucker's problems."

"Awesome. I'll talk to mine as well."

He jerked his head, and said, "See you later," as she nodded, before she swiped on her phone and said hello.

He needed to stop being so afraid. When was he going to gather up the courage to tell her how he felt? Whether she returned his feelings or not, he needed to just be brave and let her know. After all, if Mrs. Tucker had been honest about what was going on with her, her problems could've been solved weeks ago. And no one needed to have stolen anything.

His situation wasn't exactly like Mrs. Tucker's, but... It wouldn't hurt for Nelly to know. And it would make him feel better if he just told her. Maybe there was no future for them, but... maybe there was.

Chapter Thirty-Two

*C*andlelight shimmered softly in the darkness, making the atmosphere of the church feel magical as snowflakes fell gently outside the windows. This time, the atmospheric choice was intentional, since the electricity was not off, but Roland and Nelly had decided that to have the entire service by candlelight would give a special feel to the entire thing, and enhance the holiday mood.

Plus, back when Jesus was born, whether it was in the winter or not, there definitely was not electricity.

Not that turning the lights out for one evening gave anyone the idea that they were similar to biblical times, but it lent a shimmer of authenticity to the Christmas program.

Roland had been instrumental in helping Nelly work through her pre-program jitters, joking with her, and easing her fears.

She didn't know why she always got nervous. It was up to the children to do well, not her. She couldn't force kids to learn their lines or parts.

Still, as co-directors, it all came back to Roland and her.

But she needn't have feared. Robert McBride, Roland's nephew, did an amazing job as Joseph, delivering his lines perfectly, and Nelly suspected that Roland had gone over them with him more than once.

Maryellen had also done an excellent job as Mary, and little Lilly shone as a silent angel.

Even though angels were all men in the Bible, American tradition seemed to typically cast them as female, and Lilly excelled in her role, looking angelic and sweet.

At the end of the play, Pastor got up and spoke a few words, just an invitation to the congregation, reminding them that the heavenly family always had room for one more who was willing to accept Jesus's finished work on the cross as atonement for their sins, and accept His free gift of salvation, which He offered to all who would believe. It was the only way to heaven, since Jesus said He was the way, the truth, and the life, and no man came unto the father except through him.

It was a beautiful message, short, to the point, and a perfect end cap to a beautiful play.

The pastor emphasized the baby in the manger being God's gift to humankind, just as salvation was a gift, not something that could be earned or paid for.

It was also the reason that tradition had evolved for people to give gifts at Christmas time, in imitation of the gift that God had given to them.

Nelly had thought about the Secret Saint, and all the different things that she and Roland had done that season. They were all gifts, freely given. No payment expected or even wanted in return. That was what a gift was.

But, she supposed that she did enjoy seeing people appreciate her gift, and then, she appreciated even more seeing people use it wisely.

At the very end of the service, Pastor had gotten up and announced that the perpetrator of the stolen money had been caught. He also said that she had expressed remorse, and asked for forgiveness. Pastor said a few words about forgiveness, and how we were to forgive others as God had forgiven us. It wasn't a large step from there to the fact that she had been granted forgiveness, and had said that she was going to be paying everything back.

Pastor had no sooner said that when Mrs. Tucker stood up.

"I can't sit here and allow Pastor to say that without admitting that it was me. I was the one who was stealing the money." A ripple went through the crowd, and Nelly stared at Mrs. Tucker. She had not expected this.

"I did say I was sorry. I did ask for forgiveness. I'm ashamed of what I did. And while I felt like I had reasons at the time, I offer no excuse." She swallowed hard, and Nelly knew this had to be exceptionally difficult for her.

"I wanted to publicly apologize to Roland McBride. I had cast aspersions on his good name, knowing that his reputation was such that he probably would not be formally charged. I also knew that he could probably shake it off, and I knew as well that there was no evidence that linked him to the crime, so he could not possibly be punished for it. I thought I was doing a good thing by picking someone who could not be connected with a crime, but I realize that instead of allowing my good name to be soiled, I soiled his. There's no excuse for that, and I'm sorry."

The sanctuary was completely silent, as the echo of Mrs. Tucker's voice faded away.

Nelly for one couldn't contain her astonishment. She knew her mouth hung open, but she couldn't change it. Mrs. Tucker had apologized. She had done so in such a way as to make Roland look good, while making herself look bad. It took a very big person to do that.

And, from the look on her face, she didn't expect the congregation to offer forgiveness as much as they offered judgment and condemnation.

But, as Nelly continued to think about it, Mr. Johnson stood up in the back. "I think everyone should have compassion on you, Mrs. Tucker. You've been through a very difficult time, having lost your husband recently, and it never even occurred to me that money might be tight. I'm sorry about that. I admire you for taking the blame, and making sure that everyone knows that Roland wasn't involved."

Soon another man stood up and said basically the same thing. Until the entire congregation had not only stood up, but had started moving toward Mrs. Tucker, taking turns, hugging her, and telling her that it was okay. That they forgave her.

Nelly found herself swept up in the crowd, and even though she had already told Mrs. Tucker that she didn't hold it against her, she moved towards her, to give her another hug.

"What a brave woman you are," she said, when it was her turn to stand in front of Mrs. Tucker.

"Not brave. Forgiven. Redeemed. But still sinful."

It was a simple answer, but it was true for everyone. Nelly couldn't judge Mrs. Tucker, unless she wanted someone else to look at her life and judge her. She certainly wasn't perfect.

Her eyes swept the crowd, until she saw Roland standing with his mother, still waiting to talk to Mrs. Tucker.

He had been looking at her, and when their gazes met, he smiled.

There was no bitterness or anger on his face, and she knew that he had completely forgiven Mrs. Tucker. Especially after what they had agreed to do for her.

After tonight, Mrs. Tucker would find out that all of her debt had been paid, and if her son still moved in, the money he paid in rent would be extra income for her to supplement her small Social Security check.

The thought made Nelly smile wider, as Roland stepped up, and wrapped his arms around the older woman.

Maybe it was Nelly's imagination, but it seemed like Mrs. Tucker gave him an extra big hug.

"Congratulations on such a wonderful program. I believe that's the best Christmas program I've ever had the privilege of attending," Kelsey Trainer broke into Nelly's musings.

And before she knew it, she had a line of people waiting to talk to her and congratulate her. She made sure that she told each of them that Roland had done just as much if not more than she had, because she could not take credit for the Christmas program herself. Roland had definitely made a difference.

It was another hour until the sanctuary cleared out, with the last person speaking to her being Pastor, who had thanked her for taking the program on along with Roland.

He didn't realize how difficult that had been for her to begin with, and she was grateful that she had made the decision to say yes anyway.

Her life had changed over this Christmas season, and Roland was the reason.

As Pastor walked away, she realized that Roland had been standing to the side, although she didn't know for how long.

"You put on a good program," he said softly, as he strode to her, the candlelight still glittering in the windows and the sound of the congregation enjoying the refreshments downstairs drifting up as a muted, cheerful background noise.

"That's what everybody's been saying, and I keep saying the same thing: I couldn't have done it without you. You had just as much to do with it as I did, if not more."

"I don't know about that, but I'll definitely share in the credit."

She laughed at how he said it.

"But that's not really what I wanted to talk to you about," he said, as he finished closing the distance between them, and stopped in front of her.

As she had been talking to all the other people, she'd been slowly putting costumes and props away, as had he, and now, they stood at the front of the church, done for the evening, as she blinked.

"What did you want to talk to me about? Some Secret Saint activity we need to do tonight yet?" she asked, glancing around the sanctuary to make sure that they were alone. If they were going to be talking about the Secret Saint, she didn't want anyone overhearing them.

"No. I wanted to talk about how I feel about you." He grinned a bit, and tilted his head. "I'm not used to saying things like that. Or talking about how I feel."

"Okay," she said carefully. Was he saying what she thought he might be saying? Because she knew exactly how she felt about him, and she'd been thinking about telling him for a while.

Could he feel the same? Or maybe he just wanted to tell her what a great friend she was. The idea was a little discouraging. She didn't want to be a great friend. Although, that wasn't true. She did want to be a great friend. She just wanted to be more. So much more.

"I guess I could start at the very beginning, which is actually before that Valentine's Day when I said those things I didn't really mean, and started the whole thing."

"It was my fault. I didn't have to take it so badly, and hold onto it for so long."

"I'm trying to talk here," he said, grinning, humor in his tone.

"I'm sorry," she said, laughing.

"No. I was teasing you. Because this is hard, harder than it really should be. I just wanted you to know that I think I'm falling in love with you. I've enjoyed working with you, and... I didn't mean all of those things I said back then either. I had a huge crush on you at the time, and I think that it's only gotten stronger."

She held her breath. He seemed to be wanting to say one more thing.

"Nelly, I love you. I understand if you don't feel the same—"

"I do. I love you too! Everyone I talk to says that they thought our antagonism and competition was just that, me masking my feelings because I was secretly attracted to you. And maybe it was. I know for sure that I've never worked with anyone I've gotten along better with, and not only do I love you, but I admire you, and how you handled things with Mrs. Tucker just confirmed everything I thought about you."

Maybe she said more than she needed to, but he had been listening, drinking in her words like he was hanging on every syllable, and enjoyed hearing her.

"So... Would you like to spend Christmas at my house tomorrow?" he asked softly.

"I'd love to. Except... My gram." She was downstairs with the other ladies. From what Nelly had seen, she had been lucid all evening.

"Her too. Of course. My mom would love to have another lady her age there, maybe it will help take everyone's mind off of her, and help her as well."

"I'm sure her grandkids will help with that, but if you don't think anyone would mind?" She paused. "I'd love to spend Christmas with you." She'd love to spend the rest of her life with him.

As though he read her mind, he said, "I'd love to spend the rest of my Christmases with you. I don't want to push too hard, but I'm not playing. I am looking at a serious relationship that ends in marriage in the not too distant future. Does that scare you?" he asked, and grinned a bit, almost as though he were afraid of her reaction.

"Far from scaring me. That makes me happy."

"Nice." He hesitated just a moment and then said, "It would make me happy to kiss you."

Her smile filled her face. "I was so upset when we got interrupted the other day while we were delivering gifts, and you passed up the perfect opportunity to kiss me. I thought that meant you didn't have feelings for me."

"I thought I was being a gentleman."

She laughed. "Maybe you were, but I think there are certain times in a woman's life where she doesn't want her man to act like a gentleman."

"I'm your man?" he asked, his head lowering towards hers.

"I think that's what we just established."

"Hmm." He said. "I thought we just established that I was going to kiss you."

The light shimmered, and laughter drifted up from downstairs, as he leaned closer and his lips settled on hers.

She couldn't think of a more romantic setting, and she couldn't think of a better outcome for the Christmas program. And then she quit thinking, and just enjoyed the feel of his lips on hers, his hands on her back, the cords of his neck under her fingers, and a sweet spirit of Christmas swirling all around.

Chapter Thirty-Three

Christmas morning

Roland stepped up on the porch in the pre-dawn light, excited about seeing Nelly again. True, he said goodbye to her barely eight hours previously, but... it felt like forever. They'd been texting in the meantime, but he couldn't wait to see her in person, to be able to put his arm around her, greet her with a kiss. Say Merry Christmas to her hopefully for the first time in a lifetime of Christmases together.

He had his hand raised to knock when the door opened.

Nelly's face stretched with a huge smile as she stepped forward after opening the door and said, "Merry Christmas!"

But she didn't stop. She came directly to him, and wrapped her arms around him.

He lowered his head and gave her a Christmas good morning kiss.

It was better than the ones he remembered from last night. And he was smiling as he lifted his head.

"I wanted to come two hours ago. But that made it worth it."

"I was up two hours ago. You could have," she said, as he clasped her hands and they looked into each other's eyes.

He supposed they were in the early part of a relationship where everything seemed fresh and new, except they'd been working together for a while, and he really knew her. He knew she was the kind of woman that he had been looking for all his life.

He just didn't know if she thought he was the kind of man she wanted.

"Well there he is. I could have told you that the two of you were going to get together." Gram came to the door, her purse over her arm, and a coat making her look all snug and warm.

"Really? 'Cause I really didn't have the assurance that she even liked me, yet alone that we'd end up together," Roland said, offering his arm to the older woman, and smiling as she took it.

She batted her eyes up at him, and almost sounded like a young girl when she said, "If I were younger, I'd have been after you myself."

"Gram!" Nelly said. "I couldn't let you have him. He's mine."

The ladies argued a bit over him, as they walked to his truck. He had told Nelly he would be there in the morning so that he could drive them to his family's house where everyone would be gathered by eight o'clock to spend Christmas morning together. They'd be eating breakfast, working on making a meal, and teasing each other about gifts. They'd probably even open them too, although that wouldn't really be the focus of the morning. They'd read the Bible story together out of Luke, and sing carols, play games and be together.

He loved their Christmas morning traditions, and was excited to be able to share them with Nelly.

She and her gram fit right in as his family arrived shortly after they did.

His sisters welcomed Nelly with open arms, and even Isadora, who had a lingering sadness around her eyes, seemed exceptionally cheerful.

The kids running around made it a happy chaos, and the idea that there would be more babies next year added to the anticipatory feeling in the air.

But, Roland's eyes were mostly on his mother. She seemed... happy. Totally at peace. Even joyful.

Meanwhile, in his mind, he was thinking this could be the last Christmas they all spent together with her. He wanted everyone to know, so they could savor it as he was, but she had specifically asked for no one to be told, and he had honored that promise. He hadn't even told Nelly, although he wished he could have. He wanted her to tuck these memories of his mother away. They were important to him, and he thought that Nelly respected her as much as he did.

Still, the atmosphere was joyous and celebratory and they had a great time, eating and singing, and opening gifts and playing games and just fellowshipping with each other.

Nelly glowed. His mother had hinted that maybe it was the glow of a woman in love, and Nelly had agreed wholeheartedly.

He thought it was just the way she always looked.

Later, after the celebration, and they had eaten their meal and cleaned up the dishes and played more games, Gram seemed to be nodding off on the couch, and he leaned over and suggested to Nelly reluctantly that maybe they should take her home so she could nap.

Nelly seemed just as reluctant as he to say farewell to everyone, but they did so in short order and indeed once they got home, Gram went straight to bed.

Which was fine with Roland, because as much as he loved the boisterous atmosphere of his whole family being together, he enjoyed sitting on the couch with his arm around Nelly, her pressed to his side, as they talked about everything and nothing at all and somehow they both seemed to assume that their relationship was going to end in marriage. He knew that was what he intended, but it was gratifying to know Nelly felt the same.

"Do you think we'll be able to continue to do the Secret Saint once we're married?"

"Of course," he said easily and then he paused. "But... Maybe it would be a good idea to try to hand it off to someone. Just in case..."

"We have children?" Nelly finished and while her cheeks reddened a little, she didn't look embarrassed. "I do want kids. Lots of them. Maybe ten."

"I think we need to draw the line at six," he said, not really caring whether they had six or ten or twenty, if that's what Nelly wanted.

"Regardless, it might be hard to continue the Secret Saint activities with a growing family."

"I agree completely. We should probably be looking for someone to pass the baton to." He didn't think there was any rush, although he did have a small box in his pocket, and he had been considering asking her a question all day. On one hand, he thought it might be premature, on the other, he was pretty sure he knew her answer. After all, they were talking about marriage and children. And neither one of them were dating to mess around. They were dating with the intention of getting married.

"I have a friend who might be taking the a position at the school here in Mistletoe Meadows. She's unmarried, and with her position as counselor, she would have access to all kinds of great information, even if there was some she couldn't share for privacy reasons.Still, I think she would be a good candidate to consider."

"She sounds perfect."

"Do you think we should try to find a man to do it with her?"

"I know that having you do the Secret Saint with me made a big difference for me."

"Same. There were so many things I wanted to do, but couldn't, and we were able to pool our resources and do so much more together than we could do apart."

He thought about marriage. Wasn't that what that was? Two people coming together and becoming more than the sum of the two of them. They made each other better, they encouraged and helped the other person achieve more than they would have been able to achieve on their own. Those were just some of the many benefits of marriage.

Secret Saint partnerships were not exactly like marriage, but... it worked the same way. People became more than the sum of themselves alone.

"I definitely think that's something to think about. But we have to make sure that we get two people who are compatible. If...if we had known who the other was at first, we might not have gotten along so well."

"That's true," she said with a laugh. "I can't believe I ever thought anything bad about you. You've totally changed my opinion and without even trying to."

"Same for you. I didn't expect to like, get along with, fall in love with Nelly Bushnell. But I have."

She beamed.

And, without giving it a second thought, he put his hand in his pocket, took out the little box, and then slipped off the couch and onto one knee.

"Nelly, I know this is crazy fast, but... I love you. Will you marry me?"

He probably should have prepared a speech, had all kinds of wonderful things to say about how the moonlight shone on her hair or something, but he got out the words that were important, anyway.

From the look on Nelly's face, he'd done okay. She practically radiated joy, as her hands covered her mouth, and then they slipped around his neck as she hugged him and said, "Yes! A thousand times yes!"

He laughed, because she hadn't even given him a chance to put the ring on her finger.

She pulled away after a lingering kiss, and he said, "I don't know if it'll fit. It belonged to my grandmother. She lived with us for a while, and I'm not sure why she entrusted me with her wedding band, but she did."

"I didn't even look at it," Nelly said, looking at the delicate golden band he held. "It's gorgeous."

He loved that the ring wasn't the most important thing to her. It was him. He was the most important thing to her, and she couldn't have been more obvious about it.

"I can have it resized if it doesn't fit," he said.

"That's fine. And I'm honored to wear her ring," she said as he slipped the ring on her finger.

It glistened in the light, and looked perfect on Nelly's finger, at least in his opinion.

"I couldn't have picked out a better ring if I had had a million to choose from."

He felt like maybe he had done the right thing. And interestingly, he didn't have any qualms at all about marriage. At one point he might have thought that it was a huge step, and he'd never ever be able to make a decision without a lot of fear and trembling. But, this felt like exactly the right thing to do.

"I love you," she said, putting her hands on his cheeks and looking into his eyes.

"I love you too. Merry Christmas."

They spent the rest of the afternoon curled up on the couch, talking about plans and hopes and dreams and how soon they could possibly plan a wedding, what kind of wedding they wanted, and all the million things that a couple in love talked about.

It was the best Christmas he ever had.

❄

Join Jessie's list and be the first to know about new releases and sales on her books!

Read *Candy Cane Dreams*, the next book in the Mistletoe Meadows series, where Kate arrives to heal children's hearts—and unexpectedly finds her own healing in a struggling candy shop, a silent little girl, and the warmth of a small-town Christmas. Will love be the sweetest gift of all? Keep reading for a sneak peek now.

Kate Woolbert tightened her grip on the steering wheel and watched the snowflakes as they fell lazily down, drifting up and over her car windshield as she drove through the sleepy town of Mistletoe Meadows.

The street lights, with large lighted outlines of Christmas trees, candy canes, or snowmen anchored around them, made the snow glisten and glitter as it slid past her car as she motored slowly down the street.

Everything she owned was in her car, although she wasn't thinking about that as she looked at the dark storefront windows that somehow, despite the early hour and the lack of anyone walking around, still managed to seem warm and welcoming.

She left Baltimore shortly after midnight because she hadn't been able to sleep. She still had several hours before she was supposed to meet with Principal Stevens about her new job as school counselor, which started after the holiday break. But since her old job had ended at the end of November, they had agreed that she could spend the month of December hanging around the school, helping where she could, and getting to know the teachers and students and their parents.

It was the kind of opportunity that existed only in a small town school.

Small towns.

She looked again at the sparkling Christmas decorations, the cheerful, yet dark, store windows, and wondered again how she'd ended up here, because she didn't really think of herself as a small town girl.

A light caught her eye, something a little different, a little warmer than the rest, and she looked across the street, her gaze catching on a cute, weatherbeaten sign in the shape of a candy cane. Then she looked below the sign to the yellow light that had caught her attention.

Behind the counter, a man—impossible to tell his age from where she was in her car—stood at the counter, dumping ingredients into a large mixing bowl. A white apron was tied around his waist, with a picture she couldn't discern, but she guessed probably had something to do with Christmas on the front of it. It was faded and worn, and yet somehow still cheerful and Christmasy, even though she couldn't see the details.

Someone was up early this morning. As early as she was.

Although he hadn't driven from Baltimore. He was happy, content to do his job in an old store in a small town, where he'd probably lived all of his life.

It wasn't something she ever saw for herself, but... somehow the idea of living in a small town didn't seem quite as repulsive as it had through her teen years and college years.

Her roommate, Nelly, had constantly raved about the amazing close-knit, family-like atmosphere of her small town. But Kate had been determined that she would remain a city girl. After all, teaching in an inner city school for an impossibly low wage was one way to give back to her community, wasn't it?

Her car inched down the road, and she lost sight of the man in the window as she pondered that question. It didn't feel like she was giving anything back. The things she was teaching at the inner-city school didn't really help her students at all, and she wasn't allowed to talk about her faith. Not even a word. And yet, she could tell them all kinds of lies about genders and sexuality and despicable things that went against every moral code she might have, and it was perfectly okay. How was that serving her children?

It had become a moral dilemma for her, and then the terrible breakup last Christmas of the engagement that she thought was going to lead to a happily ever after for her had ripped everything out from underneath her, and she had started applying for other jobs in other communities, although... again, she wasn't sure she wanted to be a small town girl.

Somehow, she found herself in a parking lot at a church at the edge of town. She turned around and started driving back through, ostensibly looking for places for rent.

Baltimore's high rents and low wages had left her with very little savings, and she needed someplace cheap and fast.

Her savings would dwindle exceptionally quickly if she had to stay at a hotel for very long. Not to mention, the closest one was forty-five minutes away.

She turned around and tried to justify the second trip through because she needed to find a place to stay, and she might have missed a for-rent sign.

But deep down, she knew it was because the town made her feel like she was curled up in an ugly Christmas sweater, a mug of cocoa in one hand, a fire blazing in the hearth, as she read a good book and the Christmas tree twinkled in the corner beside her.

How did a town give a person a feeling like that? She never felt like that in the city. But she loved the hustle and the bustle and the busyness and the fact that there was always someone awake, and she never felt alone. Weren't small towns lonely? And dead? Boring?

The yellow lights of the candy shop caught her attention again along with the man, still behind the counter, still working, still doing what he always did, she supposed.

This time, she noticed the elaborate candy cane display in the window and the sign that said "Handmade Candy Canes."

Did people actually handmake candy canes?

She didn't even know that was a thing.

But the store just seemed so cozy, the display so blatantly Christmasy, and the man obviously content with his work. He wasn't on his phone, and he didn't even look up as her headlights flashed by.

What would it be like to be so grounded and rooted in one's life?

Kate set the feeling aside. More than likely, small towns were not for her, but it would be a nice change of pace, give her a little bit of something to put on her résumé to beef it up some, for the time when she got her next job at a big school in the city.

And not as an assistant counselor, but as the head counselor.

She told herself she had to familiarize herself with the town, the people, and the things that they did. Now she knew there was a candy cane shop in town, and a man who was up early to get started making something unique.

By the time she rolled through town again, she hadn't seen any for-rent signs, but the place was starting to come to life and dawn had started to break over the top of the eastern foothills.

The Blue Ridge Mountains were to the west, although the town was high enough up that she felt like she was living on one. Maybe they were. She didn't really do a whole lot of research into the topography; she had to admit that she was surprised to see snow in Virginia this early in December. Who would have thought?

Certainly not her, although when her college roommate, Nelly Bushnell, now Nelly McBride, had taken her home for holiday break one year there had been snow the last day, if she remembered correctly. The whole family had gone out and played in it, and Kate had joined in with them, but at the same time she had felt like it was a little... juvenile.

She still had another thirty minutes before she could conceivably show up at the school, and even then she would be early. Parking at the church where she'd turned around twice, she got out of her car, being sure to lock the door since it contained all of her worldly possessions, and then started walking up the street slowly, taking big lungfuls of the mountain-scented air. It felt crisp and cool and somehow cleaner than the air she was used to breathing. Was that a thing?

It had to be in her imagination. Air wasn't cleaner in small towns. Cities had done an outstanding job of becoming more environmentally friendly and Baltimore hardly ever had to deal with smog or anything of the sort anymore.

"Kate!"

Kate turned around at the sound of the female voice. She thought she recognized it, and a smile took over her face as she saw her good friend, Nelly. Now Nelly McBride. Nelly had gotten married over the past year, which had been bittersweet for Kate, since she had also planned a wedding for earlier this year, except last Christmas, her fiancé had called it off. On Christmas Day morning. Of all times.

Shaking those bad memories out of her head, Kate returned Nelly's hug, listening as Nelly introduced her husband, Roland McBride.

"It's good to meet you," she said, shaking the hand that had been offered.

"Nelly always talks about what a great friend you are. Sounds like you guys had some fun times in college."

Kate smiled. Nelly had been a fabulous roommate, kind and considerate, and while she had always been up for a good time, she'd also been a great study partner as well.

"Those were the days," she said with a small smile.

Nelly nodded. "I was so bummed that you weren't able to make it to our wedding."

"I'd had that mission trip scheduled for years, and I didn't want to miss it." Her heart had always been in helping underprivileged people, children especially. But lately she'd begun to wonder if maybe the way she'd been helping ended up not really being much of a help. Giving people things never seemed to make them better. And in fact, she'd seen real life data that had shown that when children were given things instead of having to earn them, it made them worse.

That study was one of the many things that had gotten her thinking and had inspired her to resign her job and apply for other jobs, including the one here in Mistletoe Meadows. That, and the fact that Edward had broken up with her.

"Have you found a place to stay yet?" Nelly asked, her head tilted slightly to one side, her eyes sparkling with joy and happiness.

It was amazing how being with the right person could do that to a person. Nelly just seemed to glow.

Kate pushed down the little frission of jealousy that threatened to steal her peace and happiness.

She was happy. Of course she was. She was starting a new job in a new town. She had been hired over all of the other applicants, and Principal Stevens was excited about the job that they were going to do together.

And so was she.

"No, I haven't. That was part of the reason I was walking around town. I thought maybe I had missed a sign or something. Are there no places for rent here?"

"The market is tight, that's for sure," Roland said, his voice sounding grave and serious.

He and Nelly looked at each other and seemed to nod a bit before Nelly turned to her and said, "But you could stay with us. We're living with Roland's mom right now, and my grandma moved in too. But there's plenty of bedrooms in that big old farmhouse."

Nelly was going to go on, but Kate put a hand up, cutting her off.

"That is so very generous of you, but I couldn't possibly impose on Roland's mother's house."

There was no way she was going to take her up on that offer. A person just didn't do things like that. It was one thing to go home with her for a couple of weeks over the holidays. That had been bad enough, but to move in with newlyweds and the groom's mother? And some other woman? No way.

"Seriously. We'd love to have you. And there's plenty of room in the house."

"If you don't mind my siblings dropping in once in a while. We're all family there. My mom will probably put you to work too."

"I couldn't imagine living there without working. But of course, I would pay rent, except..." She couldn't explain that she had very little money, but it also just went against her sense of what was right. Because she could see that Nelly really wanted her to. Would that be so terrible? Her moving in with Nelly and her husband and his mom and their grandma?

Yeah, they seemed sincere, and maybe things were different here in a small town versus where she grew up in the city, but in Kate's experience, people really didn't want to be imposed upon like that.

So she rebuffed Nelly's efforts to get her to change her mind, firmly saying that she would spend more time hunting for a place to stay.

"Then at least stay with us until you find a place. It would be cheaper than a hotel."

"That's very nice of you. If I don't find a place by the new year, maybe I'll take you up on it."

Nelly looked disappointed, but she nodded.

The new year was a month away; surely she would find a place by then.

"If I can't get you to stay, at least come for supper tonight," Nelly said, smiling and giving her an appealing look.

She had already said no to the offer of lodging; she could hardly turn down supper. Although, there was still that part of her that didn't want to impose.

"You're not going to be putting anyone out. There's always plenty of food. No one's going to cook anything different if you come. There's just... friendly faces and hearty food." Roland didn't seem like he was begging her, but he was simply laying out the facts. Did he really not mind people descending on his house?

"You talked me into it," she said, still unable to believe that it wouldn't be an imposition. At the very least, they would have more dishes to do.

"Awesome. We'll see you tonight at six. Does that work?" Nelly said, her eyes shining like Kate had just given her a hundred-dollar bill, rather than an agreement to eat supper with her. Maybe Kate was looking at it all wrong.

She tucked that thought away for later. It was possible that she was mistaken, although she had been raised to give other people a wide berth and respect their privacy and family. Again she thought that maybe it was the difference between growing up in the city and growing up in a small town.

After a little bit more small talk, they parted ways, with Kate going back to her car and heading toward the school.

As she passed by the candy cane shop one more time, she glanced in the window and saw a little girl staring silently at the man, who appeared to be talking.

Other shops were open on the street now, and the town had, if not come to life, at least started to wake up.

Maybe that little girl would be at school in a bit, and perhaps Kate would meet her, along with all the other children.

It was going to be a big difference from the school that she had been at, a much smaller student population. Less than a quarter of what it had been at the inner city school where she had worked.

In one way, she was looking forward to possibly knowing the name of every child, which Principal Stevens had assured her every teacher and administrator knew.

Kate somehow found that exciting and unbelievable at the same time.

Regardless, a little thrill of excitement went through her, for the change if nothing else, as she got in her car and headed toward the school.

Sign up for Jessie's newsletter! Get a free book, access to exclusive bonus content, get fun and funny updates on her life on the farm and more!

A Gift from Jessie

View this code through your smart phone camera to be taken to a page where you can download a FREE ebook when you sign up to get updates from Jessie Gussman! Find out why people say, "Jessie's is the only newsletter I open and read" and "You make my day brighter. Love, love, love reading your newsletters. I don't know where you find time to write books. You are so busy living life. A true blessing." and "I know from now on that I can't be drinking my morning coffee while reading your newsletter – I laughed so hard I sprayed it out all over the table!"

Claim your free book from Jessie!

www.ingramcontent.com/pod-product-compliance
Lightning Source LLC
Chambersburg PA
CBHW031036310726
48969CB00007B/2002